Parisian Reasons

AN HOMAGE TO HEMINGWAY'S
A MOVEABLE FEAST

Jay Snyder

goldenretrievermedia@gmail.com
© 2014 by Jay Snyder
All Rights Reserved

ISBN 13: - 978-0-9892153-1-2
ISBN: 0989215318

Other Books by Jay Snyder

RETRO SKETCHES: A MUSICAL DIREC-
TOR REMEMBERS

KEYBOARD RESULTS: PIANO AND FUN-
DAMENTALS FOR EVERYONE, VOL-
UMES 1 & 2

GOLDEN RETRIEVER MEDIA

Parisian Reasons

Jay Snyder

Editor: Dan Marcus

Cover Design: Maxine Cameron Stenstrom

Back Cover Photo: Mel Weinstein

Café Illustration: Brielle L'Étudiant

CONTENTS

PREFACE

Things have been left out. Some were magicians' secrets I can't reveal but everyone knows. The less discreet will probably do a reality show someday and ruin it for *Cadabra the Great*.

I didn't talk about *La Plume de Ma Tante* [The Pen of My Aunt], a café where stunning women — all writers — served as waitresses just to pick up life experiences. Nor of trying to incorporate another author's stream of consciousness: "Bless the mess, the duress, and this crummy preface." Nor the difficulty we had trying to find a restaurant behind the Notre Dame because I couldn't properly pronounce "The Burning Log" in French. No talk of the expensive red sweater that was too flashy for my personality. Nor the night when we were trying to eat *steak-frites* and a band of vegans swept by and spray-painted my meat. The book would be richer with these details but they were edited out. As they say in Paris, *"Quel dommage."*

Jay Snyder

Carpeteria, California
2014

NOTE

Nobody knew where Jay Snyder was — or if they knew, they weren't saying. Reports had been circulating for months that he'd been spotted in London or Amsterdam. One correspondent claimed to have seen a man who looked like Snyder sporting a beret, walking along the Seine. I could discount that rumor immediately because I know for a certainty that Snyder doesn't own a beret. I was beginning to suspect that he had finally made good on his casual vow to vanish from the face of the earth and devote his life to writing works of literature so deep, only he'd be able to understand them.

Then, on a misty morning, an email arrived from Snyder, dateline: Champagne. I was relieved to receive it because I hadn't heard from him in months. He stated that he would be in the States next week and wanted me to meet him at Dagwoods, a charming pizza restaurant in Santa Monica where we'd convened many times when he was working on his previous books.

I was sitting at our customary corner booth when he walked in the side door behind me that led to the small patio on the street side. He was cordial but distracted as he glanced at the menu. He smiled slightly and said that he couldn't stay, but would send me a postcard in a few days from Paris. Then he placed a large envelope in front of me. I undid the clasp and pulled out the manuscript it contained just far enough to see the title: "Parisian Reasons." I asked him if this was "the book," and he responded that it was "a book." He wished me "Happy *Oktoberfest*," then, as suddenly as he appeared, Jay Snyder was gone. A few moments later he re-entered Dagwoods, this time through the front door, and ordered a stromboli to go.

The book you are holding in your hand or viewing on your digital device is not the book I was expecting. His contract clearly specified a work of fiction, not an extended piece of reportage describing his experiences on the continent both physical and spiritual. Aware that bloggers had long noted Snyder's uncanny devotion to Hemingway, I was at least relieved to see this was not the book I feared most: an opaque monograph on trout fishing in the halls of Shambala.

And he did send me that postcard as promised: a glorious shot of the Arc de Triomphe. I instantly understood, and soon you will too.

- Dan Marcus
Editor

I don't see how a man is to be good for much unless he has some one woman to love him dearly.

- George Eliot

A MUTEABLE BEAST

Paris. It brought out the beast in you and that beast was changeable. If you had three or four drinks every day — conforming to an Internet definition of alcoholic — more beast.

I was sitting in a warm café. It was spring and women were wearing falsies to attract men. Even though I was married, I could look couldn't I? Why don't they open a window? I'm sweating like the buck on the Jägermeister label.

My laptop was in a small bag I carried. I hoped the bag wasn't effeminate because my wife didn't want me to use a purse but I needed something for the computer and this was the best I could find. From Peru, made of fabric, it was orange and olive. Looking at it made me hungry so I ordered.

"What's good today?" I asked the waiter.

"Nothing is good, monsieur. We just went from an 'A' to a 'D' rating. Didn't you see the sign in the window?"

"I didn't notice. What happened?"

"The health inspectors found out our tuna sashimi was really canned sardines from Maine."

"That seems so obvious."

"Not if you don't know the difference."

"I really like it here. Everyone is so absorbed in laptops or cell phones and there's lots of privacy. I can write without distraction."

"Except for the women with falsies."

"That is so true. How is it you're so perceptive and yet a waiter?"

"This is not what I really do. I'm a songwriter."

"What songs have you had on the radio?"

"None."

"So you're an aspiring songwriter."

"Have you decided what you'd like to order?"

"Well, since the food's bad, I'll have a bottle of... do you have a good California Pinot noir?"

"In Paree, monsieur?"

"Sorry. Sorry. How about a large carafe of *Château d'Yquem*?"

"A dessert wine at seven-thirty in the morning."

"I have a sweet tooth. Do you have the 1847?"

"Oui, monsieur. It is twenty-three thousand, five hundred and twenty-nine dollars. As of last night...on eBay."

"Make that a Bud Lite."

The waiter nodded politely and went to fill the order. I turned my head to avoid looking at the falsies so I could write. I opened Microsplotch Verb, hit the center function for the title, and fixated on the blinking cursor. If only those girls would leave, I wouldn't be so distracted. Did I have Attention

Deficit Disclaimer? I should get tested but I really didn't want to know.

I looked at my fingernails. They were dirty. I typed "Dirty Fingernails," defeated the centering function, justified left, and began:

Rick enjoyed clawing at the Upper Peninsula dirt behind his grandfather's hunting cabin because his mother told him not to.

This was not a manly story so I hit "command A," the screen turned blue, and I deleted what I wrote. Deletion made me think of my wife who dropped my last hard drive with all my backed-up work. When she broke the news to me she began laughing. That grew into a paroxysm, and before you knew it tears of derision were dripping into her morning coffee. I knew she didn't care about my stories because they hadn't made any money yet but it was cruel of her to laugh at me and think so little of my early writing and of all my writing for that matter. But why complain? I had married her because she was beautiful in so many ways.

The waiter came back. He placed an unopened can of Bud Lite on the table.

"Are you sure you don't want a *pression*? A beer on tap?"

"Pression. That means they press the hops to get the beer out, right?"

"I am not a Franco-etymologist, monsieur. I really do not know."

"That's all right. I'll have the Bud." And with that the waiter reached over and popped the top for me. Foam gushed onto the table.

I drank the whole thing in two gulps. A sixtyish man wearing a ripped jean jacket peered at me over his Costco reading glasses but I didn't feel judged. I felt a slight buzz and motioned for the waiter to bring me another beer and some red wine. I went back to thinking about titles. This is what I came up with:

> *About War but Symbolic*
> *Bull Meat for Pedro*
> *Bad Spring in a Mattress*
> *Ten Bowls of Borscht*
> *Upstate Wine*
> *The Sun Gave Me a Sunburn*
> *Jerks with Short Lives*
> *To Have and Then Not Have Anymore*

Nothing was hitting me so I chugged the second beer. I had a white foam mustache. As I wiped it away the waiter returned with the wine. A title came to me so I ordered quickly.

"I Hear Your Name, I Leave for Maine" would be about a guy who, helplessly in love with a woman, crosses the ocean to go to Barnacle Billy's in Ogunquit, eats lobster, and tries to find happiness through food.

The waiter brought more wine. The man in the jean jacket had ordered a heaping plate of hamachi sashimi that was really intestine-disturbing escolar and was now standing nervously in front of the locked men's room door. The women wearing falsies had left in search of security. The waiter took off his apron and finished his shift. And I was feeling good about my new story.

LIVING ABOVE A TIRE SHOP

Living above a tire shop had advantages. The screeching sound of air guns at seven in the morning eliminated the need for an alarm clock. And although we didn't have a car, if we ever got one....

The piercing sounds began. I went to the stove and warmed up milk for Mr. Thumby, my young son; Marcel, our small white poodle; and the missus who said cold milk spoiled the heat of her morning coffee. After taking care of three fussy freaks, I dressed and walked to a little room I sometimes used on the rue Écrire where I could write without distraction.

Walking up seven flights of stairs was exhausting but the slivered view of the Eiffel Tower was worth it. Besides, it was the cheapest unit in the building. While I was catching my breath, I built a small fire and took out some Minneola tangelos I had in my coat pocket. There were a lot of seeds. No wonder they were on sale. I sliced the hybrid in half with my penknife, sucked on the citrus, and started spitting seeds into the fire. They made a crackling sound and distracted me. Before I noticed, an hour of spitting and crackling had gone by.

I decided to make today's story about something I was familiar with: building fires and spitting orange seeds at flames just to hear the sputter, then smelling the burnt orange odor. No, that's too self-indulgent. It doesn't go anywhere. Something better was needed like...like running into another writer at dinner last night. I'd call the story "Living Above a Tire Shop."

Both my stomach and I agreed it was time to eat. Gambling at the track that week had not gone well but I had received a check from Craigslist for some rewrites I had done for them and felt I could splurge a bit on dinner while my wife and son had Doritos and Pepsi.

The rue Perdu had some good cafés — not evil cafes where horsemeat was served — but good cafés where you could drink without it being a big deal, and eat a little something too. Running into Fitzy was dumb luck because I don't like to eat alone. I like to write alone but not eat alone. But there was one drawback. Fitzy had his wife,

Emelda, with him and she didn't like to share. That meant I would have to order my own dessert.

I never met Hamlet's girlfriend, Ophelia, but if I had she would have reminded me of Emelda — a wacko. She drank too much. She ate too much. She was a hedonist but she was what Fitzy needed. Maybe she wanted too much in the bedroom too but I was never to find that out. I only witnessed the fallout of a man who couldn't write anymore once Emelda turned him into a zombie.

We exchanged pleasantries. He asked me how my writing was going. I said "fine" and we ordered. They chose the vegetarian chateaubriand and I settled on the mock blowfish with French fries. House salads came with each meal so I had the French dressing and they went with the French Colonial dressing.

All three of us were pretty hungry so we said nothing until dessert. When Emelda's pear tart came and I asked for a bite she grew strangely withdrawn.

"*Mai non*," she said pretentiously.

"*Pourquoi?*" I asked.

She had run out of French so she switched back to English. "Because it is so little and I don't know if you have any hanker sores."

"I'm married."

"But your wife could be seeing someone while you're at work."

"That's unlikely. She loves me."

"I love Fitzy but what about the pool boy? Why don't you try the Key lime cheesecake. There's a dessert not to be trifled with; much better than this little tart."

I knew a sow when I saw one so I let the matter pass. Fitzy tried to lighten the conversation. "It's good to see your stories are coming along so well. When are you going to start a novel?"

The thought of a novel frightened me. *War and Piece,* about prostitution in the Russian Revolution, was almost 1,400 pages. *Notes from the Underbelly* was a best-selling diet book but I didn't know any weight-loss gimmicks. *Withering Heights,* about the discovery of Viagra, was a good idea but it had been done. I love dogs but *Old Yeller, A Dog of Flanders, Rin Tin Tin,* and *White Fang* had all been adapted or adopted, and I was not the kind of writer who could knock out a *Black Fang*. After dinner, drinks were served. What took so long? The conversation grew livelier.

"Cats. Are there any good cat books out there?" Fitzy asked.

"That's a good question. I had a cat so I know cats, but..."

"How about a cat that falls in love with a bat? They're about the same size. It could work. You could call it *The Cat in the Bat*."

"Are there any reported instances of cats boffing bats?"

"You'd have to do the research," said Fitzy.

"I'm not sure there's an audience."

"Okay, okay. Wait. You live near a church, correct?"

"Yes."

"And it has a loud bell that rings right before Sunday mass, right?"

"Right again."

"Okay. Could you use this: *For Whom the Bell... Makes a Big Racket*"?

"The title needs work."

"Wait. Wait. Here's a better idea: An old, decrepit fisherman goes to sea in his broken-down little boat. He's at the end of his rope. If he doesn't catch something substantial he's out of business, ruined. But he catches the biggest tuna on record. He thinks he's got it made but that night, skin diving sushi thieves cut big chunks out of the guy's fish, leaving him with a bloody skeleton. Call it *The Old Guy and the Tuna* — a metaphor for failure in the face of persistence."

"That's the worst idea I've heard all week."

"Waiter...another round of absinthe for everyone."

"Got anything else?"

"What do you think of this: *The Sun Sets and Don't You Forget It.*"?

"I like it."

"Could be a celebration of every depressive that ever lived."

Emelda finally chimed in. "I have one more bite of pear tart. Do you want it?"

Too late.

THE EVIL CAFÉ OF
STRANGE DRINKS

Okay, so I screwed up. My wife would ride me every Thanksgiving, Christmas, and Yom Kippur: "Why did you do it?" Anherst would pout. We'd both drink too much, have a fight, and the next morning everything would be forgotten because of our blackouts. Then I'd go to an evil bar like the *Café des Ivrognes* [Café of Drunkards] where the drinks and the women were cheap — so cheap, in fact, we called them courtesans.

The bar served drinks with weird names. The *Ney Hey* was rum with Mountain Dew. The down of the alcohol and the up of the caffeine was like drinking a Baileys and coffee. Then there was the concoction of rainwater and grain alcohol called the *Strangelove*. I don't know if it was named after a movie or the Sixties' pop group but three Strangeloves put you in outer space. I mean you bumped into Sputnik, scrawled graffiti on Skylab, and pinned the tail on the Mars Rover. It was wild.

Another good one was the *Cuban Libra*, a rum drink based on astrology: freshly made rum combined with Red Bull. I had to agree with the linguists — it was freeing but it should have been called a *Cuban Taurus* thanks to the meaty mixer.

And G-d help you if you had to go to the bathroom. And you did unless your name was Gorp, the humanoid robot from the film *The Day the Earth Didn't Have Electricity for Half an Hour*. It looked like the guy who laid the cement for the men's room floor wore very big shoes (Gorp again?) and stuck his feet in the wet concrete. You'd put your feet where his feet had been, "drain the lizard" as they say in England, and get back to the bar.

This place was a dump but it was my dump. I could rarely afford better, living a life of genteel poverty. My wife's relatives were well-off, my father sent me some of his dentist money, and I had income from the Köln version of Craigslist for disguising porno ads. But like John Lennon, who really wasn't a working class hero but a middle class genius, I wanted the kind of sympathetic life story people could relate to.

I tried not to go to this café on the days when the boys' and girls' potties were emptied by a truck that was painted what the French call *merde brune.* Anyone in the neighborhood who could leave did so for a week. Those who had to stay daubed Lysol on their upper lips and bit the bullet. But when the reeky process was over, everyone returned for the cheap booze and the tall tales.

When the rains came and you were sitting in the café, warm and drunk, and you looked through any window and saw homeless people on the street getting soaked, trudging toward pneumonia, you felt the weight of the world and ordered another drink. With the walk home along the rue Napoleon I sneezed, sensed the beginnings of a sore throat, and remembered the minuscule emperor suffering on cold, damp Elba. I opened the door of my modest apartment and was glad I had a place out of the rain.

Too cheap to buy firewood or kindling, I knew my wife had an old winter coat to provide some warmth. I wore no underwear but had several sweatshirts and could sleep in those as long as there was some kind of laundering in my future. My son, Thumby, had lost his pacifier and was sucking on an ice cube. Good, I thought, he'll make a fine scotch and soda man some day.

My wife shivered so I hugged her and gave her that "let's go to bed" look. She gave me that "where's the chow?" look.

"How's this?"

I took a roll out of my pocket, she ate part, gave the rest to our son who was starting on solid food, and said with great warmth and sarcasm, "Thank you." I felt ashamed and went back to my evil café.

"Bartender, give me a *Trader Moe's Headache*" — a fifty-cent bottle of wine with four aspirin. Although it reminded me of Listerine, I savored it like NyQuil.

"Where's this wine from, anyway? Not that I care."

"Upstate New York," replied the bartender. "Good, huh?"

"For a man who wants to forget...better than good...great!"

"Glad you like it. If you have four, there's a ten percent discount. Tonight only."

I ordered three more just to see if I could do it... like eating a five-pound hamburger.

"What's for dinner?" I asked.

"Five-pound hamburgers."

"What's up with that?"

"We got the idea from a French version of an American TV show. In English it translates into *Gorges, Pig Outs, and Much,* he said. *"Tout le monde aime* ça [Everyone loves it], especially when they do the split screen of children in Biafra watching."

"That seems cruel."

"Commerce, monsieur. Commerce. It makes people hungry. Then they purchase."

I felt sick but ordered another drink. "Can you change the channel?" I asked. He did and I watched an endomorphic little blonde girl with her mother — nose dripping with no tissue at hand.

"I don't believe this."

"They are happy in their world," said the bartender, and went back to filling other orders. I walked home, stopping on the way to pick up a croissant-burger for my son and wife. She was pleased by the simple things of life and I looked forward to her heart-wrenching smile.

Next morning at the same café a pretty girl came in. She wiped raindrops from her face and I was floating. She leaned an umbrella against her chair, wriggled her shoulders, and adjusted her bra straps. I was hopeful. Then she loudly blew her nose. Honk! Images of sailors, foghorns, and lighthouses appeared side-by-side in my mind like a C.S.I. lineup. I was through with her. But it didn't matter because a handsome young man with a cold arrived, wiped his nose on his sleeve when he thought no one was looking, and took her away.

I went back to writing. An idea was there and so was my appetite. First I ordered a *blasé* — a beer smaller than a *distingué* so it wouldn't draw attention. Mussels arrived next with a buttery lemon garlic sauce. All you had to do was try not to eat the unopened ones. In this evil little bar, if you got sick from eating unopened mussels they'd say you "got hep." Not jazz lingo; you got hepatitis.

The bar was owned by a lawyer so for certain dishes you had to sign a waiver in case you got sick. And your heirs couldn't prosecute if you died eating the food. My stomach wasn't gurgling so I opened my laptop and started typing.

I Hear Your Name, I Leave for Maine

Then there were the good vibrations. When she was sober she was a joy. When she was loaded she was a pie chart of monsters: Dracula (sucking energy instead of blood), the Bride of Frankenstein (impeded by a brain soaked in alcohol), the Wolfman (so changeable and a slave to his animal nature), a zombie (the walking sexually dead), the Invisible Woman (isolated in her room watching fourteen hours of TV a day), the Mummy (all wrapped up in her problems), Godzilla (that interrupting son of a newt), and Jekyll and Hyde ("The one dram experiment of Jack Daniels at 9 a.m. failed. Will try two.")

I had made the point in my story that there were difficulties with the wife of my main character. I stopped writing because I knew what would come next, grabbed my coat, and put another roll in my pocket.

THAT'S MY FLYPAPER AND
I'M STICKING TO IT

Caught myself in a lie. Wife asked me where I was last night. Told her I was at my favorite café, *Deux Pierrots*. Was really at Googi Mug's apartment drinking strong pale yellow alcohol that gave you a hell of a buzz, erasing inhibitions so I could network and advance my career as a writer.

Googi's story was fascinating. Her father had been a wealthy reverse-plastic surgeon. Beautiful women with terrible lives and hang-ups caused by all the attention their good looks brought went to Dr. Mug and had little bumps put on the bridge of their nose, bags added under their eyes, high cheekbones reduced, and bald spots created where once there had been luxurious, Vogue-y hair. When Googi was a teenager she would sit in her father's waiting room and watch the transformations from faces that launched thousands of ships to faces that sunk freighters.

When she graduated from Fleet-Anemone Girls' Academy de Berne, the selection committees from all the best colleges of the world fell panting at her feet since the parents' ability to pay was a key entrance requirement. Despite her grades, Googi attended Mount Holyoke, Harvard, and M.I.T.

While studying physiology she came up with the phrase that was self-published, became available online, had millions of hits, and made her internationally famous: *A nose is*. What a bracing breath of nitrous this was to the literary community. She taught and took her own course — The Rule of One, 101 — and flunked herself because she could.

After graduation Googi moved to Paris dispensing logic: ("Don't buy clothes, buy baseball cards"), drollities ("Less is more unless you're hungry"), and sexual theory ("Less is more unless you're horny"). I was stunned by the breadth of her half-million dollar education and sat cross-legged on her Iranian carpet drinking her Polish booze, wide-eyed like a student at the feet of Buddha, Krishna, or Kowalska. "Oh, Steinway" she would say, "sometimes I think you only come for the krupnik."

But this tilt-a-whirl salon was drawing to an end and surprisingly I would be the one to end it.

Googi had a female friend who had given herself the nickname pp though no one knew what those letters stood for. Of course, people made guesses: peripatetic pedestrian, pathetic populist, penile prude, puffed-up popcornist, Pfeffernüsse peddler, and very quiet.

One day I came to the door, the fussy French maid let me in, cleaned the door, and asked me to sit down in the foyer. I saw an offal fight going on: Googi and pp throwing sheep intestines at each other. Googi had the heart of a Trojan but today I heard whimpering.

"Don't go, pp. What can I do to make pp happy?"

"I need relief from this life. Every night I feel the pressure. I can't stand it anymore. I have to go."

Googi turned into a little girl from Jamaica thanks to a childhood vacation in Kingston.

"pp no happy? Me make pp happy. Here." And she pulled a ring from her finger and handed it to pp who promptly threw it into the fire.

"Ouch, ouch, ouch" cried Googi as she retrieved the ring from the flames.

I had a sightline to the two women but I wasn't sure if they saw me. I got up and went to the door. The maid gave me that "don't go" look but I left and stayed away for months. My wife liked that.

THE DRUNK PEPSI GENERATION

It was the *Ethan Frome* of rejection notes: "Nice but not that nice."

A New York publisher had put a Band-Aid on a stab wound with that first "nice." The L.A. guys would not even do that. Usually they wouldn't even reply or return a phone call, much less be honest with you. Since you can't predict when someone's fortune is going to turn, the safest thing to do was nothing.

After forty-seven "no's" from the gatekeepers of the printed word, I still felt I would be published and had something to say and today I said it to a bartender: "In my opinion mescal is psychedelic tequila." I got so wasted I over-tipped because I saw eight shots on the table instead of four.

People saw me as gregarious but deep down inside I was a loner. I often drank alone, only relieved myself when everyone had left the restroom, and blew my top whenever the mood struck me. This was one of the few cafés that still allowed me in.

Through my fog I remembered I had an errand to do for Googi. She'd asked me to pick up her car at *Lube Jobs de Paris*. I was drunk but I was also responsible, so with cartoon-like rubber legs I left the café and wended my way north.

An older attendant looked me up and down and immediately made a value judgment: "You are a drunk generation."

"I thought we were the Pepsi Generation."

"Okay, put rum in a can of Pepsi and you're the Drunk Pepsi Generation."

"Who orders a rum and Pepsi?"

"You're not bothered I've called your whole generation drunks?"

"Not true. Some of us take anti-anxiety meds."

"Then you're the stoned generation."

"I believe that's taken."

"The rude generation?"

"That's another group but you're getting warmer. Hold on." I took out my iPhone, somehow found the voice-memo function, and spoke: "Tell Miss Mug about the Drunk Pepsi Generation. Could be good salon fodder."

I paid for the Ford, didn't thank the attendant, spied a soda machine outside the garage, and bought a Coke.

When I delivered the car to Googi's place, pp was waiting for me downstairs.

"There's no parking on this side of the street on Thursdays from 1:00 to 1:07."

"A.m. or p.m?"

"It doesn't say. That's how they get you."

Sure enough a meter maid drove by and eyed me in the car. I pulled away and imagined she was cutting herself. I found a space on the rue Minuscule and squeezed in.

"Miss Mug would like to thank you," pp said. "C'mon up."

We walked in to the sound of laughter. Googi had deftly cued up a whoopee cushion app as the posterior of the most famous poet in Paris sat down. When the rude noises came, he turned red and didn't know whether to graciously be the butt of the joke or exude a few lines of iambic pentameter. I muffled my laughter as Miss Mug refilled the encouraged poet's glass:

> *Ere he*
>> *leave before the ebon*
>>> *mist*
>>> *of midnight obscured the rail-*
>>> *lery of the*
>>>> *day.*

Googi motioned for me to come over.

"Thank you so much for getting my car. How much do I owe you?"

"Nothing. You've done so much for me already."

She put up no fight. "Well, all right then. Would you like a drink? pp, get this man a rum and Coke."

"Googi, pp...what would you say to a rum and Pepsi?"

"Shocking. Different. Semi-original. Wherever did you come up with that?"

And I proceeded to tell them both about the Drunk Pepsi Generation.

"I can use that," she said. "You won't use it, will you? I need something to describe how certain people are these days. A tiny bit of assonance, pithy, overarching and perhaps over-reaching, but what fun to see if it gets a rise in the blogosphere."

"Go for it, Googi," I said, thinking I'll use it if her version bombs.

Walking home I had another idea that I spoke into my digital memo pad. It was the name of a character: Senator Beveridge.

After writing, it was necessary to clear my mind by watching hours and hours of television. The well of my subconscious needed replenishment from a muddled puddle of ideas pooled on the surface of the obvious.

Inside our cheap rental, the TV was loud. It was hard to hear dialogue over the wail of the air guns from the tire shop below but I didn't mind since action-adventure shows usually mixed the music too high, masking predictable lines like "freeze," "drop it," or "don't even think about it." I lay down on the bed — no couch, too expensive. My wife was absorbed in an American rerun dubbed into French called *Adam-Douze*. Twelve handsome policemen were caught in a conundrum of poor plotting. The *TV Guide* said, "A drug deal goes perfectly and everyone leaves happy." I asked my wife if I could change the channel. She made a hand motion which meant "yes, but I'm annoyed."

I left the show where it was and picked up the *Classics Illustrated* comic book, *Idealistic Marriage*. The editors had simplified it: "No matter what the husband thinks, the wife is always right."

"What's for dinner?" I asked.

"Ramen noodles."

"What did you put in it?"

"A green onion and a peach pit."

We sat down to eat. I sipped and commented, "Flavorful."

My wife smiled and turned her head back to the TV. She observed life with a great feeling of brotherhood. "It's good to see the drug lords win every once in a while."

"That's interesting. They're not having tequila at the cartel celebration," I noted. "What are they drinking?"

"Rum and Pepsi."

OTIS-PARSONS REGRETS

Before I became nonplussed by Googi's private social life, Ms. Mug and I had long conversations about books, especially the *Kama Sutra* and new ways to lose weight.

"Have you read *The Pacific Palisades Papaya Diet?*"

"I can't afford organic fruit."

"How about *The Beverly Hills Way to Attract Solvent Lovers Through Thinness.*"

I tried to change the course of the conversation. "You've read *War and Peace*, right?"

"My G-d, man, there's too much free porno now. How do you expect me to wade through Napoleon's licking when there's all that..."

"Don't you even like Tolstoy's philosophical tracts where he's trying to quantify key elements of the world?"

"Can't say I agree with them, dear boy. He says instinct trumps reason. Can you believe that?"

I could see this turning into a steam heat argument so I switched gears.

"Are you familiar with the value of *Flash #1?*"

"The comic book?"

"Some call it literature," I defended.

"Right," she said with disdain.

"Last time I checked Wikipedia, it was worth close to half a million dollars," I countered.

"And Dostoyevsky. Have they made a comic book of *Crime and Punishment?*"

"In a way. It's called *Batman*."

"I can see that. Were you one of those kids who read *Classics Illustrated* instead of the real thing and then wrote your book report?"

"No. I like books."

"What have you read lately?"

"Scanned Erica Jong."

"*Fear of Flying?*"

"No, *Fear of Cinnabon*."

"That's a book?"

"No, but I wish it was. I'd be thinner."

"What do you really read?"

"Besides the Yellow Pages?"

"Don't you have the Internet?"

"I have the Encyclopedia Britannica and 4-1-1. That's good enough for me."

"How do you feel about Marquez?"

"Fantastical."

"The Andrew Weil cookbook?"

"Delicious dishes, but how many people have access to gochujang or buckthorn juice?"

"Do you have any recommendations for a young writer?"

"Yes. The latest version of *Grand Theft Auto*."

"That's a video game."

"Right, but a big part of the culture. Go with the flow, man."

"So man's inhumanity to man doesn't interest you?"

"Women's inhumanity to women, yes. Man's inhumanity to man, no."

This challenging and enlightening dialectic continued through the early morning hours — the hours, if my wife had gotten up during the night noticing I wasn't in bed — that would lead to a fight the next day.

I thought I'd be a bit flippant to test Miss Mug's reaction.

"And so, Your Highness, anything to add to that?"

"Yes, a private, painful thought I need to finally unburden. I wasn't accepted at the Otis-Parsons Institute."

"Even with all your family's money?"

"Yes. Even with all my plastic surgeon father's dough. They blew me off."

"Why was that?"

"I had no talent."

"So how is it you're so world-renowned today?"

"It was the little phrase about the nose I thought up in college that got published."

"You do have a favorite author, right?"

"Yes, indeed. Heloise. She knows how to get stains out."

BIRTH OF A NEW L.A.

A certain kind of weather, the stillness, where and how shadows fell, the majesty of Paris when the evening lights were turned on, even the amount I had to drink and how it made me feel — all these things helped me conjure up different places at different times. Today I began to get a hazy then clearer picture of Los Angeles. Not yesterday's film noir or today's rap culture but a mash-up of *Blade Runner, Valkeries of Encino,* and a student film about an existential villain who wants to kill the world.

So it was mandated that anyone who wasn't beautiful had to leave L.A. or get plastic surgery. We read about it in the new Paris tell-all, Au Jus.

The exodus of a tiny percent of the city began overnight. Off they went to the caves of Oregon, British Columbia, and to a town many people mispro-

nounced: Carpeteria, California. They were happier too because now they didn't have to put up with the wave of rudeness that had been sweeping Los Angeles for years, characterized by honking horns, thrusting middle fingers, lane changes without signaling, cutting in line, and covetous grabbing when Nordstrom's had a teeny weeny sale. We in Paris found all of this hard to believe since "Liberty, Equality, and Fraternity Parties" was our motto. But when L.A. elected a mayor who had been a casting director, the purge was inevitable.

Sitting there in my café, evil though it was, my typing fingers could barely keep pace with my mind. I had lived in L.A. for a time and had experienced everything I was writing about. In my pocket was a vegetarian rabbit's foot — made of mock liver and a bit smelly because of its age. I rubbed the faux foot for luck and part of it crumbled because tofu doesn't hold up. I could feel fortune trickling through my hope glands as I continued:

Some of the enjoyment the jettisoned got as they left Tinkle Town was displaying one of three bumper stickers that united them in their va fanculo-ness: "There's No Business Like Blow Business," "Don't Know When I'll Be Back Again," and "Take Me To the Bridge."

The muse of Shakespeare had inserted a literary suppository and I was filled to the rim with the good taste of brim [*sic*]. Then I was interrupted by the editor of the *Transoceanic Journal*, Chevy Wallace Chevy.

"How is it going?" he began, derailing my train of thought.

"You miserable Faulkner," I said, regretting I had used a once great author's name in vain. "Can't you see I'm working?"

"Oh come now. Certainly you've got time for a drinkypoo. I'm buying!"

I let go of the story I was working on like a Pentecostal lets go of a snake that's just bit him and said, "I'll have a double Rémy Martin," which was not as greedy as it sounds since the cognac in Paris was very reasonably priced that year compared to the States. Chevy stalled for a moment, then took out a credit card and slapped it on the table. "For you, anything," he said. "Waiter, I'll have one of your delicious ice waters." Knowing that Chevy was a wine connoisseur and gourmand yet apparently broke at the time, I could see through his grimace that the conservative order was killing him.

The waiter snatched the card from the table, winked at me, and said, "I will run a tab for Monsieur." Chevy nodded, then turned to me and brought up the topic of dyslexia. Mine was undiagnosed. It was a meaningless conservation.

He leaned forward in his chair. "I've been keeping a record of my feelings since I was a child. Each entry began with the same words: Dear Dairy."

"You lived on a farm."

"No. D-a-i-r-y. D-i-a-r-y. They're easy to mix up. They look the same on paper like lowercase 'b's and 'd's."

"Were you teased as a child?"

"Oh, G-d, yes. One, because I was a Taoist, and two, because I only spoke in palindromes for a year."

"Really?"

"For all of third grade I went around saying, 'race car, race car.' "

"Did you ever get to 'Madam, I'm Adam'? "

"No. The comma threw me off. Its palindromicness wasn't perfect." I moved into his world: "Apostrophes are not commas." The waiter brought our drinks.

"What other memories about your childhood were important?" I asked, knowing I could turn the question into two more doubles.

Chevy gave a sideways glance like a liar does before answering and said, "To tell you the truth" (another liar's verbal cue), "I wanna see the sun of my childhood blotted out from the sky. My psychologist says 'things will get better. Move on.' "

"Well, I for one don't think you should move on. That's where creation lies. Dig a little further into your artesian well of pain."

"That's deep," he said.

And worth another drink I decided, and waved my hand. "Waiter?" He scurried over and I pointed to my glass.

Chevy Wallace Chevy had the same look on his face that I once had when I linked up with a girl at LAX, brought her to a Malibu restaurant, and heard her say to the waiter in her syrupy Southern accent, "Ah'll have the lobstah." But this time I wasn't paying. Chevy was. He was paying for having interrupted me and paying for being an annoyance that I had to put up with to get a decent buzz. And he smelled bad.

"So you haven't told me anything about yourself," Chevy said. "That's like making love while you're dressed and your partner is undressed."

I let that comment pass because I wanted a third drink. The floodgates opened: "My father was a dentist so I discovered Valium at an early age. My mother dressed me in little girls' clothes. I burned all the pictures but still go to sales at Veronica's Secret."

"And do you know what Veronica's secret is?" he asked in jest.

"Yes. Yes I do."

"And what is that?"

"It's called focused ultrasound. Better than liposuction."

"But I thought those models starved themselves to get that look."

"Sound waves explode the fat cells," I continued. "My wife's mother goes to one of the specialists who do the procedure. She sees those women in the waiting room and writes us about it."

I motioned again for the waiter. "Another double Rémy Martin for me and more ice water for Monsieur." The waiter looked pleased.

"Surely you have more hush-hush. What else can you tell me?"

I drummed four fingers on the table, rolled my eyeballs, pursed my lips, took a breath and said, "I'm not sure I'll ever measure up to what my father expected of me." Hearing my own devastating words, I paid for the third drink and left quickly.

WHO IS SLIVER?

Her store was a four-by-six kiosk located in a tasteful Paris mall. She sold Kindles.

When your place of business is twenty-four square feet you'd better be thin and Sliver was. A friend of mine called her "stick woman" because you could feel the bones of her pelvis as she hugged you. By her feet at all times was her bitch: George Eliot, hound dog.

Sometimes I'd jones for a browse and stop at her shop on my way home from the café. This day she insisted on fronting me a Kindle.

"I can't pay you right now."

"Oh, you'll have plenty of money soon. Don't you worry. Aren't you rewriting porno ads for the Amsterdam Craigslist?"

"That's funny. I signed 'anonymous' on my contract. I'd rather be known for my short..."

"...declarative sentences. Yes, effective. You use those for the ads, right?"

"That's correct. Man seeks waif. Subject, verb, object. It's good practice."

"So you'll have money from the ads. Then your stories will sell. Remember you showed me one about salmon fishing and another about a safari? They're superb. Then you'll write a novel. I have faith in you. You'll be rich and then all-knowing. I see it. Now what do you want me to upload for you?"

"Turidnev?"

"That's too depressing for a heavy drinker. How 'bout something lighter like *Medieval Zombies?*"

"I'm open for something new."

"Have you read *The Yiddish Buddhist?*"

"No, but let me guess: Jewish stories with a Zen twist?"

"Exactly. *Meshugge* meditations. Crazy contemplations. Here, I'll upload one for you."

I held my new Kindle and read:

A rabbi walks into a bar but not on Friday night or Tisha B'Av [a holy day commemorating the destruction of the First and Second Temples]. He says to the bartender, "Give me a glass of kosher extra-heavy Malaga wine from Upstate New York." The bartender says, "Rabbi, that's the sweetest wine on the planet. Wouldn't you rather have some Baron Herzog cabernet? It's also kosher and much drier." The rabbi asks the bartender this question: "Is learning from the Torah not sweet?" "I wouldn't know," says the bartender, "I'm just one of the mishugoyim." The rabbi looks puzzled and asks, "Then how do you know the Yiddish word for 'mixed-up gentile'?" "Well, Rabbi, I used to have a Jewish business partner and he called me that when he drank before I bought him out at an addict's lowball price." "And why did he drink?" inquired the curious rabbi. "We had too much sweet wine in stock. Someone had to drink that dreck!"

"So that's a Yiddish koan, I mused. Gives you a lot to think about."

"That's the idea."

"Ya know, alcoholism isn't funny. There are people who would be offended by that story."

"Are you?"

"No."

"Neither am I. Want a drink?"

"In the middle of the mall? In your kiosk?"

"I own it. I can do anything I want. I've got slivovitz or Jack Daniels."

"Slivovitz is a colorless liquor, right?"

"Made from plums. One hundred to one hundred forty proof."

"Let's have that."

Sliver reached beneath her neat display and without showing passing shoppers what she was doing, filled two small glasses and handed me one.

"*Nazdrave*," she toasted.

"What's that mean? Don't drive drunk?"

"It means 'good health to you' in Bulgarian."

"Where did you learn that?"

"From meine Kindle-a."

After two more shots I was feeling false positive so I turned toward my café, thanked Sliver, hugged her goodbye, rubbed at a sharp pain I suddenly felt in my groin area, and moved like a wired lab rat through a maze of streets till I was sitting in front of my laptop resuming my story about the future of L.A.

They had passed a law. No lawyer was allowed to be a lawyer without first taking an extensive, exhaustive, conclusive test (it paralleled the MMPI[*] so popular with psychologists and psychiatrists) to assess the morals of the subject. Ninety percent of aspiring lawyers flunked. This cleared up so much jetsam in society it was astounding. Frivolous lawsuits became a thing of the past. Legalistic ploys that extended billable hours or allowed people to get away with murder ended. Everyone except landlords who rented space to attorneys was happy.

But you had to take the good with the bad. Neon flourished. Starbucks put the sexist breasts back on the corporate green mermaid logo and made them bounce like a burlesque dancer's. Bacon-only restaurants tried to outdo each other neonically with wiggling pork fat. L.A. citizens either became too coffee-hyper or too large from all that delicious

---

[*] *Minnesota Multiphasic Personality Inventory*

bacon: *bacon-wrapped steaks, bacon ice cream, spaghetti alla carbonara, and bacon sushi.*

In the end it wasn't "beauty killed the beast," it was trichinosis. The only ones left to rebuild were Orthodox Jews. The city went back to wearing black — not much of a stretch — and everything shut down on Friday night like it was Tel Aviv. Civility returned. Instead of those L.A.-isms like "cool," " dig it," "chillaxin'," and "homies," we heard "nu," " vos machts du," "Shabbat shalom," and, of course, "oy gevalt" because the world was still not perfect.

NOT REALLY SALMON FISHING

When Rick got off the train he could see there was no more town. Black now and I don't mean in an R&B way, but burned to the ground black. It didn't matter. Rick picked up his fishing gear, slung an L.L. Bean knapsack over his shoulder and walked northwest to the salmon stream he had known since he was ten.

The iPhone in Rick's head played songs you or I wouldn't know. His songs.

When he got to a place he recognized except for the burned-down trees, he decided it was time to eat again. Breakfast had been what he thought was a healthy granola bar, but when Rick read the ingredients he saw "high fructose corn syrup" and retched. Rick knew hunger.

Laying his pack on the cold, cold ground, black from the terrible fire, Rick took out some freeze-dried tofu and a bottle of General Tso sauce that normally went on small bites of fried chicken except that Rick was a Pescetarian. He made a fire, ringed it with rocks, and laid a sauté pan on top. He shook the General Tso sauce into the pan and it immediately started to sputter like an old Szechwan cook trying to explain in English to a skeptical customer that there was no General Tso. It was all made up — a culinary fabrication like Springfield, Missouri's cashew chicken. No one in the Fu Mao province of northern China had ever heard of cashew chicken or General Tso for that matter. A good reason to go to a burned-out town on a salmon fishing trip: to escape the lies.

The fake sauce was bubbling and the tofu — better if it marinated overnight — was turning from soybean white to phony Tso brown.

Rick knew he had to wait because sputtering meant very hot and he could burn his tongue like he had done in Rio Nido on habanero s'mores; a burned tongue meant he would be lisping but there was no one around to point that out. In the end Rick waited for his fake food to cool down and ate it.

For dessert Rick thought fruit would be a wise choice. He pulled a silvery packet of desiccated peaches out of his pack, ripped open the "cut along this line" part that never went well, drizzled a bit *of water over the barely recognizable genus Prunus, and watched peaches come back from the dead. He was saving a desiccated hot fudge sundae for later.*

The ground smelled like a thousand unfiltered Camel cigarette butts. Rick took a stick, scratched at the earth like a hedgehog until the ashtray odor went away, laid some pine boughs on his resting place, put down a tarp, a painter's drop cloth, and his sleeping bag, then went to sleep thinking he'd overthought this.

To see the sun first thing in the morning is invigorating. But Rick overslept, tired from something. He snatched the bottle of General Tso sauce and put on his reading glasses: "Soy sauce, ginger, high fructose corn syrup." Rick made a sad Sarah Silverman clown face, paused artfully like Conan O'Brien, then cursed like Seth Rogan: "Those muckers!"

Rick had several ways to make coffee. He chose the one an Israeli cab driver taught him — instead of boiling sugar with the grounds, he used a sugar substitute found on the Internet called monk fruit powder. It tasted a little better than sucralose and a lot better than that bitter stuff his father used to put on grapefruit called Sucaryl. Rick was a diabetic.

Rick drank the Mideastern brew, spitting out little brown bits of grounds. No one was around so it wasn't impolite or gross. After all, "if a bear goes in the woods and there's no one there is anyone bothered?"

Rick's teeth were now full of little black dots resembling cavities. The thought to floss passed through his mind but was overruled in favor of rinsing in the salmon stream.

Rick put out the fire by recycling internal water from his two birds/one stone playbook, gathered his equipment, and made his way to the stream. It was just as he remembered: flowy. Porno salmon were fu...spawning, and Rick wanted in on the action. Taking out his rod he put a hook on the end of the line and thought about what lure to use. Someone who ate tofu would not stick a sharp, painful hook into the thorax of a live grasshopper so Rick got out a small red spinner. The color reminded him of the Sixties. Where had all those colors gone?

The striped lure hit the water and made a splash. Nothing happened. Fishermen get used to that just like songwriters. I'll keep working it until those flipping salmon get here, Rick thought. Just then a breeze came through like the one he felt that day back in town before it was reduced to a blackened flat plain of nothingness, like pizza with shoe polish sauce. Rick remembered walking into the 9200 Building on Sundowner Way. Or was it the 6255

Building near the old bank? The location wasn't clear but the memory of the breeze was. It was a refreshing breeze that gave back energy after you'd been up all night working. Rick smiled, remembered a meeting in one of those buildings, and spat. "You flubbers!" he mouthed and continued fishing.

The sun baked Rick like a three hundred and fifty degree rotisserie working on a skewered Costco chicken. Besides being hot, Rick was also hungry. "Heat, food, heat, food" went the obsessive-compulsive chorus in his head. Lunch won.

In his right pocket was a garlic sandwich. Rick was too poor even for onion, let alone lettuce or tomatoes. On top of that, the bread was stale, so Rick dunked his low-level lunch into the cold stream making it worse but he had no choice — he was hungry — and ate the soggy mess with a mixture of gratitude and hatred.

A strike! The salmon must have smelled Rick's garlic breath or enticing crumbs may have floated to hiding place depths. Whatever the case, Rick was thrilled to know he'd be having fish for supper. This was a big salmon so one was enough. Rick didn't need to be a pig like people who took too much, logged too much, mined too much, ate too much. He jammed his knife into the salmon's gut, slit sideways, threw the awful part into the stream for the raccoons, filleted like a low-paid expert in a high-priced fish market, and took his prize back to camp.

Rick kept kosher so he had no bacon to grease the pan. He reached into his pack, felt around and came up with a plastic bottle. He sprayed some "I Can't Believe It's a Food Product" into his sauté pan. Not surprisingly, it didn't act like butter or oil. It coagulated like the demonic chemical concoction that it was. Still, better than nothing.

Tshhhh. The fish hit the pan and started to turn from red to pink. Lemon would be good, so would salt, but Rick had foolishly forgotten these simple, easy-to-carry ingredients, opting instead for kasha and groats.

Stillness. The salmon tasted good and he had gotten his omega-3 fatty acids for the day. Rick yawned, lay sideways on his sleeping bag, quickly went through his mind's Rolodex of wrongs done him and happy moments too. As he stared into the fire and started to nod off, he felt satisfaction at the job he'd done burning that hurtful town down.

SNOW JOBS OF KILIMANJARO

When you've married a woman with money, you can go on safari, kill things, and then die a bit yourself knowing you haven't done your best writing-wise, and then die again knowing you deserve it. I deserved it because those animals I shot at didn't have a gun to shoot back at me, and because I drank two week-old scotch all afternoon — she wouldn't let me have the good stuff — and I couldn't write anymore due to my drinking.

"K'wimbe," I shouted. "Bring me another scotchysoda."

"But Bwana," he politely replied, "Missus bitchy say no more drinky for Bwana."

"Well you tell missus that Bwana need more scotchysoda so he forget numbness in leg from thorn attack and bickering from bitchy wife. You tell her that, will you?"

"Yes, Bwana, but bitchy wife tell K'wimbe no more scotchysoda for Bwana because K'wimbe got fie dolla from missus bitchy and that more than Bwana give K'wimbe."

"Listen, you larcenous bugger, you bring that drink or I'll put on an endless loop of the Kingston Trio singing 'Scotch and Soda' and stop filling out your Social Security paperwork or whatever the bleeding heck you call it here in Nairobi or Kenya or wherever we are."

"Si, Bwana, ya. Two languages good enough to let you know I dig where you coming from. And me not judging, Bwana. You want straight up...neat, or with ice cubes that delay the fog you so crave."

"You know what I want, you clucking lackey. Just get it. Ice or no ice, I don't care. Can't you see? I don't care about anything. Me leg's gone gamey. All because I didn't put Bactine on a simple little wound made by a thorn. And I may not be able to feel my leg but I can feel sorry for myself for not writing about the one real thing I saw this morning: Zambo-oloo, one of the bearers, taking a three-minute leak with the longest uume I ever saw." What could I write about this python? It would give women who read "National Geographic" nightmares, make normal men feel shame for the way G-d made them. No. I couldn't write this true thing because it was too true. If I had a contact at 'Ripley's Believe It or Not' I could have written a few words, but how would they handle the illustration? What newspaper would run that? Everything was a washout today. Then there were the vultures — waiting. Waiting.

Scotch takes you to places you've never been and makes you see things differently. You get insights but they're snow job insights. For instance: the name of the mountain I've been staring at all bloody day. Kill-a-man jaro. And I'm the man to be killed. Plucking thorn.

Actually "jaro" could mean "greatness" and "kilima" could mean "mountain." I'm just mucking with you — another snow job constructed with the adult Tinkertoys of a glass, ice, and cheap scotch. What else is there to do while you wait for death or the Thai food you ordered two weeks ago that couldn't possibly come yet will still appear on your credit card. Hahahahaha. Dammit! Can't anybody take a joke?

"Since my leg is completely numb let's have some use of it. K'wimbe, I need something."

"Yes, Bwana?"

"Do you have any colored chalk?"

"Yes, Bwana."

"Then I want you to make concentric oval circles on my bad leg."

"Me no understand, Bwana?"

"I want you to draw a bull's-eye target on my leg."

"Why, Bwana?"

"We're going to have a little game of darts. See, here in my pack I've got regulation darts, just like in the pubs back home."

"Me against you, Bwana?"

"Yes, and you don't have to pretend to lose."

"Do I win something?"

"What do you want?"

"I want to watch Zambooloo take a shower."

"Why?"

"I want to see his uume."

"That's not very manly of you, K'wimbe. Can't you think of another prize?"

"Yes, Bwana."

"Well, what is it, man?"

"K'wimbe ashamed, Bwana."

"Out with it!"

"Well...Bwana...would you stop talking about your leg and death and vultures and just get on with it."

"Hmmm. You know you're right K'wimbe. I too feel ashamed. Why don't you take the first shot?"

K'wimbe warms up making short horizontal motions that go back and forth. With a guttural "unh" he lets his dart fly, hitting the big toe of Bwana.

"I believe I felt that. (Bigger) I be-lieve I felt that! K'wimbe, get Mrs. Bwana. And while you're at it, bring two...no make it three scotchysodas."

K'wimbe asks, "Who third drink for?"

"Why, it's for you. We're celebrating the partial end of self-delusion."

"Why only partial, Bwana?"

"Because we're still drinking, that's why."

A pleasing ending

"K'wimbe, go and pull that dart out of my big toe before I get another infection. And K'wimbe, ask Zambooloo if he's got any herbs or bark to chew on. I'm starting to feel like my old self again."

My ending

"Listen. The engines. The plane's come to take me to (a) hospital where they can fix my leg."

"Captain, do you want some tea or scotch before we leave?"

"No thanks, old man, better get going."

Once the plane took off I could see wildebeest — the Big Mac of the Serengeti — running from lions, hyenas, and zookeepers. Then there were puffy white clouds that looked like they came from a can of Reddi-Wip. Just kidding. I'm dead. I died.

FISHERMEN AND BOOKSELLERS

Through the luminous early morning light of Paris, I walked along the Seine thinking to myself, what's wrong with high fructose corn syrup, anyway? They put it in everything.

The *bouquinistes* were just beginning to open up their meager stalls and set out their wares with the romantic river as backdrop. What looked like very old books and artifacts were displayed in dusty bins or hung from wires. A large hand-drawn, hand-colored page of music manuscript caught my eye — a single page of Gregorian chant, cut from an oversized book. Because of four strugglesome high school French teachers or my lack of language gifts, all I could do was piece together two words as cowboys did with Native Americans in John Wayne films.

"Ce vieux? This old?"

The French can be polite but above all they like to enlighten — Robespierre — and this bouquin-iste wanted to teach me something. He looked to his left and pointed to the Notre Dame Cathedral, completed in the middle of the twelfth century.

"*C'est vieux.* That's old."

Europeans are aware of and appreciate age in a way Americans do not. The world they grew up in is hoarier and their history courses not the unpleasant slogs that ours were with *farblungit* [lost] gym teachers emphasizing dates instead of events they knew nothing about.

"*Je comprends.*" I had a tiny bit of French stored up but only for words like *comprendre* and "comprehend" — obvious linguistic counterparts I recognized thanks to a good Latin teacher. I was now out of vocabulary so I pointed to the parchment and asked, "How much?"

The old bookseller scrunched his mouth into an unintentional frown and nodded his head up and down for tense seconds.

"Ninety euros."

That seemed like a good deal, and haggling made me uncomfortable. With the rolled-up manuscript under my arm I continued my walk along the bargain-imparting river.

To my right were fishermen. Being easily distracted I stopped to talk to one of them in my pathetic French.

"Vous êtes un fisher-homme" I stated ineptly because I couldn't think of the word for fish.

The proud simple man gave the smile of one who has lived a hard life. I knew he was fishing, in part, to feed himself because his pension had evaporated years before. A long bamboo pole held a delicately baited hook and line. His was a labor-intensive lot as he tried to tempt dinner with flicks of the wrist. Anchovies were useful in a Caesar salad and necessary in a puttanesca sauce, but as a main course you needed quantity — a three-inch fillet only contained about two grams of protein — and cleaning this tiny fish was no day at the beach. I cursed the greedy world that had impoverished this man, took a nerve pill, and walked on after wishing him good luck.

There was one more bookstall. This one was farther away than the others. I felt sorry for the isolated bouquiniste until I started rummaging through his wares.

"What is this?" I asked with much surprise.

"This is a porno book," he said in reasonable English, "from before the Internet."

I picked up a dog-eared copy of *Peyton Place* and with the steamy windshield memory of a teenager turned to page 284. The characters Rodney and Betty were right where I had left them, trampolining off each other's half-clothed bodies.

"Would you like to buy the book, monsieur?"

"No thanks. I've read it. I even have one of the paragraphs memorized."

Ah, the honking horn of youth.

I couldn't take it anymore and left. If my wife was in the mood, that would be great. In case she wasn't, I stopped and bought some bootleg Quaaludes from film noirish, pencil-mustached, beret-wearing Pierre. And a jug of *Côtes du Rhône*.

———

Waking up happy is a good feeling. I made coffee, and before my wife got up I was out the door and off to see an antiquarian I passed on my way to the *Café des Coqs Calme* where I wrote in the morning. As I entered his shop, *Les Choses Anciennes*, the bell attached to the top of the door made a tinkle and he emerged from behind a black backroom curtain wiping brioche crumbs from his beard.

"Bonjour, monsieur."

"Bonjour, monsieur. Comment sa va? Et blahblahblahblahblahblahblah."

Once he started answering in rapid-fire French, I was lost and needed to bring the conversation back to English. I pulled out my Gregorian bargain from yesterday.

"Is this worth anything?"

He shook his head "no." "Ah, monsieur, I hate to disappoint you but this is not so old. Do you know music a little?"

"I've had a few lessons."

"Then you know how many lines there are on the staff."

"Five."

"Yes. And how many lines does your manuscript contain?"

Here we go again with the didacticism, I thought, but decided to play along.

"Five," I replied.

"And do you know how many lines music originally had?"

I was thinking how useful this information would be if I ever decided to get a Ph.D. at Julliard.

"I give up."

"Four. Four lines before it evolved to five."

"You mean at one time it was Every Good Boy Does, and that was it?"

"Exactly, monsieur. The five-line staff appeared in the thirteenth century."

"So you're saying this is not that old?"

"It depends on what you call 'old.' "

"Phooey."

"Don't take it so hard. You thought you had a page of true Gregorian chant?"

"Yes."

"Did you know his close friends called Pope Gregory, 'Greg'? "

"Fascinating. What's this thing worth?"

"On a good day, maybe fifty euros."

"Do you think I can return it?"

"To a bouquiniste? Never."

On the walk back to my café along the river of no return, I glanced at the porno bookseller.

"Pervert," he yelled.

I continued past the place where I purchased the phony Gregorian. Only six hundred years old. I'd been had. But before I could descend into complete darkness, I found myself singing a line from a Johnny Cash song, slightly revised: I tickled a man in Reno, just to watch him laugh.

That cheered me up, and I resolved that my page of manuscript would look good framed on the wall of a future guest room.

THAT PARIS COLD

That Paris cold made the tips of my fingers numb as I swung my legs out of bed. I gently touched the cheek of my wife but her sleeping pill was still hard at work. In the quiet of the morning before her day of companionship TV began, I'd write. She was either severely depressed, lowly motivated, or both. It didn't matter because I loved her.

I boiled some water for coffee. In Europe and the Mideast they call this method *filtre*. You put a paper cone in a plastic or ceramic coffee dripper, add two tablespoons of coffee, and slowly pour boiling water over the grounds. A bit of half-and-half or hot milk with about an eighth teaspoon of sugar, and you have a pretty tasty cup of joe.

Sitting down in my easy chair, I took my laptop, opened the file I was working on yesterday, put my feet up on my navy blue hassock, and was luxuriating in morning silence when the TV blasted on. The volume zoomed up and *Les Femme au Foyer Gâtés de Lyon* [The Spoiled Housewives of Lyon] blared with barnyard yacking:

"No."

"Oui."

"No."

"Oui."

"Vous êtes une imbécile."

"No! Vous êtes la fou."

So ended my morning of peace. If I stayed away from the apartment long enough I'd also avoid *Feuding Fishmongers' Wives of Marseille* and *Scary Plastic Surgeries of Ile Saint Louis.*

In the exquisite quiet of my favorite café, I laid my silvery laptop on a brown, well-worn wooden table carved incorrectly with the initials F.U. and tilted the screen to a vertical position when the waiter came over.

Affecting round black glasses and a funny way of talking like a Jerry Lewis character, he said, *"Où est la bibliothèque*? That's all the Frensch [*sic*] I know."

"If you don't speak French, why did they hire you, and why do you want to know where the library is?"

"Oh, is that what it means."

"And your waiter job?"

"My uncle owns the place."

"How do you manage when Parisians ask you questions or place an order?"

"My uncle taught me one phrase and I use it over and over: *Tout est bon ici.*"

"Everything is good here. Clever. I like that. Okay, I'll order in English to keep things straight. I'll have a rum St. Monica."

"*A cette heure, monsieur*?"

"Yes, dammit, at this hour! I thought you didn't speak French?"

"I attend three Frensch AA meetings every week. I hear that phrase all the time."

"Well what the freak is wrong with three shots in a cup of coffee?"

"There's no room for the coffee?"

"Okay Father Theresa, I'm no angel. I write better when I'm a little buzzed. Haven't you ever heard that about writers?"

"I *have* heard that. It's among the hundreds of reasons alcoholics use to drink."

"Do I need to go to another café, *garçon?*"

"*No, garçon.*"

"*Monsieur!*"

"*No, monsieur.* One rum St. Monica coming right up."

The waiter walked away and I wanted to take his oral temperature with the wrong thermometer but I held my temper, looked at the blank screen, clicked on the centering function, and began typing:

Everything Is Good Here

The larceny at this track was not to be believed. Right before a race you could see the trainers going ape, force-feeding caffeine-rich Pepsi or Diet Sprite to the poor horses that really preferred Red Bull. By the time they got to the gate, the neighing, whinnying, and snorting made a terrible racket and only the most corrupt official could not see that these horses had been monkeyed with.

In my left pocket I kept my stash and in my right pocket I kept my winnings. If I wanted a hot dog — what the French call a "chaud chien" — I would take the money from my winning pocket. After several winners I might move some euros to my left pocket. And if I had the guts to walk away from the track when that pocket was bulging, my wife and I would have vacation money for skiing in Austria this coming winter. But if arrogance and false knowingness got the upper hand of my pocket, then I would eventually leave the track in shame and try to drink away my agony, drown my lack of self-control in a pool of Pernod, and scald my self-reproach with a hot gin punch.

"Monsieur would like to order lunch?" asked the vexatious waiter, breaking my concentration.

"Well, since everything is good here, I'll have a cheeseburger."

"I am sorry, monsieur, but we are out of cheese."

"Out of cheese...in France? Well then get me a simple hamburger."

The nutty waiter avoided making eye contact with me and looked at the floor. *"Chevaline,"* he whispered.

"Horsemeat?"

"Yes, sir. There's a losing jockey leaving the kitchen just now. I over-heard him say, 'Take that, *Sea Brisket.*'"

"That does it. Bring me the check."

"Why don't you let me buy you another drink?"

"Fine with me."

"Another triple?"

"Hit me with your best shot glass."

I drank my breakfast *and* lunch, left a hefty tip for "Jerry" and hungered for some real food, knowing my wife hadn't cooked anything and would still be watching TV when I got home.

But as a rich friend used to say to me without knowing my situation, "It's all good."

PINKY'S DOME

Pinky, a talented artist and friend, was the first of our crowd to shave his head and grow a goatee. I think he did it as a PR gimmick to attract attention. Though his pictures were quite good, he wasn't achieving the fame and recognition he desired, and I could see that was eating him up.

We ran into each other at the *Café des Étages* where I didn't write; this one was just for partying. Tequila was already on the table.

"Hello, my friend, how are you?" he said as I took off my worn overcoat, shook his hand, and sat down. "I'm fine. The work is going well. How are you, and who are these two pretty ladies?" He gestured so I could tell them apart. "This is Fatima and this is Shadowska. They're the models I'm currently working with."

"Nice to meet you, girls. How do you like working for Pinky?"

Fatima answered first, complaining like a five-year-old by accenting the last word of each sentence. "Sitting still for six hours is *hard*. Everyone thinks modeling is *easy. Il est difficile.*"

The other girl jumped into the conversation. "*Très difficile.* If a fly lands on your nose, you can do nothing. *Rien.*"

This was good. I was getting a solid grounding in the French language.

Knowing Pinky had an active libido, I made an educated guess. "But after a long and difficult sitting, does he not give a very thorough massage?"

The girls began to titter.

"You can see tension on a face," observed the painter. I do the best I can to help my models relax."

More tittering.

He continued, "Would you like to have a game of billiards with the girls? Stickball? Doctor? Get lost in the tunnel of love?"

The symbolism made everyone at the table uncomfortable except for Pinky, who was way ahead in the game of Chutes and Shooters.

Shadowska got up and left, saying to Pinky, *"Vous êtes lard."*

Pinky looked puzzled so I helped.

"I think she meant to call you a pig but she really said, 'You are bacon.' "

"She'll be sitting for me by tomorrow. Just let her go."

Fatima either hooked on the side or was thicker-skinned.

I didn't like that Pinky was pimping his girls. I knew how to get women if I wanted them. But right now I was in love with my wife. My concern was for Pinky. His paintings were as good as everything else around. My favorite was his ex-wife lying in bed with a big pillow behind her head. She was a beauty and he captured that. I knew it was maddening for him not to be acknowledged, hence the drinking. He had taught at one time and there can be satisfaction there if you allow it in. Or you can spend a lifetime feeling unfulfilled.

We ordered absinthe and were carried away by a pale green, reality-destroying mist. There was nothing more to think about that night besides having fun.

WITH A FRIEND AT LE CHIENNE

After Ping-Pong we were cooling down and discussing literature.

"*Mad Magazine* influenced me the most," I said. "I've been on the lookout for foibles ever since childhood."

"You do like to make fun of things."

"It's just my opinion, but when I see something not quite right, I have to write about it."

"Did you watch any reality shows last night?"

"I love life but I hate reality."

"What did you watch?"

"I didn't. I read a few chapters of Betty Ford's autobiography."

"Are you enjoying it?"

"I didn't like the 'not-drinking' part. What are you into these days?"

"*The Wines of Burgundy.*"

"That sounds good. Enlighten me over a bottle or two?"

"*Absolument.*"

We decided to drink outside. Year-round Christmas lights lit the trees. The white-painted wrought-iron chairs were cold against your back but encouraged you to warm up with alcohol much like the salty peanuts trick that makes you drink more beer. The café had another gimmick: transvestite waiters, all of them ex-husbands. They called the place *Le Chienne.*[*]

A server came to our table and I couldn't help thinking that depilation on her upper lip might bring more tips.

---

[*] Given that all the waiters were male transvestites, management felt that the male article, "le," was more appropriate for *The Bitch.*

"How may I serve you?" he asked without anger or bitterness.

"We would like a bottle of... anything with extra reversatrol.

"You mean resveratrol. How about some Nuits-Saint-Georges?"

"Great. We'll have that."

She turned and walked away swinging her hips.

"Live and let live," I said.

"I agree," Bevan muttered. Bad teeth kept him from really opening up.

Our serving person returned with two bottles. "We have the '81 or the '82. Which do you prefer?"

My friend and I spoke at the same time: "Both!" Then we got into the spirit of the place — "owe you a Coke" — and laughed.

He opened both bottles. "We'll let them breathe, yes?"

"Absolutely," I said.

She hadn't gotten five feet from our table when I did my impression of John Lennon counting off the song "Yer Blues" on the White Album: "two... three." Then I poured.

Our eyes went wide. Bevan spoke first. "This is the most delicious wine I've ever tasted."

I took a drink. "I agree."

This was a wine you did not slug down — a wine you treasured like a kind-hearted woman.

"What do you taste?" my friend asked.

"I taste Gaia. I taste the earth."

"I'm reminded of Italian women: complex and passionate."

Now the wine was bringing us into a harmless argument zone.

I asked, "Aren't all women complex and passionate?"

"You don't remember my ex-wife, do you? Add 'sneaky' to your list. Did I ever tell you what happened at our wedding?"

I shook my head "no."

"My future wife prearranged something with the minister. When I thought he was about to say 'you may now kiss the bride,' he said, 'all criticism ends here.' And it did. Being all bottled up I started drinking." He reached for the wine.

An attractive, well-dressed woman at the next table turned to us and asked, "No fights tonight?"

"I don't think so," answered Bevan revving up, leaving his misogyny in the dust.

There was a roped-off area close by, somewhat like a boxing ring. On certain nights, ex-husband transvestites and their divorce lawyers who hadn't achieved big enough settlements went at each other. Bloodier than arbitration, the ex-wives loved it.

We were halfway through the second bottle when talk turned to injustice.

"I heard from the bartender they're going to fire our server."

"Why?"

"She won't get rid of her mustache."

"Why would that be a big deal to him?"

"In her culture, hair on the upper lip is considered sensual; it imparts a tickling sensation when kissing."

The server came back and we both stared at his upper lip.

"Will there be anything else?"

"Just the score, thanks."

She placed a small piece of paper on the table. I took a peek as a gambler peeks at his final card in a game of stud. I lost this hand. $2,400 before tip.

I called the waitress over. "Is this correct?"

"Yes it is." He delivered the next line like Bela Lugosi portraying Dracula. "That was very old... wine."

Remorse welled up inside me. I took out a credit card used only for emergencies. My wife had two trust funds with one tied to this card. I would now have to cut back on important vices like gambling and drinking. Not good.

Bevan and I got up. I lifted the tab again just to convince myself that this was not a bad dream. Our server had drawn a big smiley face and written below it, "Thank you. Signed, Georgy Girl."

When I got home, guilty thoughts about the cost of the evening plagued my mind. I thought I'd better write something quickly about that delicious, expensive wine and hope an accountant could deduct some or all of the bill if my observations ended up in a story. Each bottle gave ten sips apiece so I wrote out the numbers one through ten and put down these observations about Nuits-Saint-Georges:

1. Mysterious perfume
2. Slightly bitter aftertaste
3. Smooth, then makes your mouth tingle
4. Even though it's only 13 percent alcohol, has a soft, warm buzz
5. Floating on a cloud
6. Better than anything I ever found at Rite Aid
7. Tiny bit of bitterness still there but now who cares?
8. Think I feel warmer
9. I hate to repeat myself but please see #3
10. All gone, Mommy. Still a little bitter but so was life with you.

ESAU GRAMM AND
HIS BEL PAESE

He may have been both adored and despised but without the blue editing pencil and generous spirit of Esau Gramm, the world would have been without many works of literature and poetry that time and Wikipedia stamped "good." So helpful was he to others, I decided to try and make him a better bowler. Gutter balls. Ten frames of zilch. But from his game of zero came a generous idea.

"Follow through," I yelled, "so you don't hurt your back and the ball doesn't bounce when it hits the lane." But his mind was elsewhere.

"Let's get Laidlow out of McDonald's so he has time to write. I love his stuff and I think he's distracted by his flipping life."

Esau was talking about P.V.C. Laidlow, an aspiring poet.

"How will he live if he doesn't have a job?" I asked.

"We'll take up a collection."

"Can we afford that?"

I didn't mean to insult my friend's financial situation, but I knew the only money he made was doing parties on weekends as DJ Mozzarella.

Esau pursed his lips, pulled at his goatee a few times, and then had his eureka moment.

"We'll make and sell cheese. People love cheese."

Throwing cold water on a rainmaker's idea is not good for morale so I let him continue.

"What's the most popular, in-demand cheese in Paris?" he asked.

"Bleu cheese for dressing?"

"No."

"Swiss cheese for party platters?"

"Well, that's Swiss isn't it," he said in a bor-
derline mocking tone. "But you're getting closer."

"Kraft Singles for grilled cheese sandwiches?"

Esau picked up the ball.

"What kind of cheese do they use on a *Croc-
monsieur*?"

"*Emmentaler*?"

"Yes, Emmentaler: the Holy Grail of Swiss
cheese.

I could see the wheels turning as he continued.

"There's a huge market for Emmentaler, and
yet there's another kind of cheese that's just as
good. Maybe better."

"What's that?"

"*Bel Paese*. It means 'beautiful country.' "

"In Italian. It's an Italian cheese. You want to
make and sell an Italian cheese in France?"

My information and logic didn't seem to impress Esau. He continued: "I've travelled in the Lombardy region of Italy where Bel Paese comes from. It can be compared to the French Alpine cheeses — tastes buttery, smells milky, is semi-soft. We could easily overtake Emmentaler with a little clever marketing.

The cheese train had arrived and I was about to board.

Esau smiled broadly. "If we had the milk brought in from the country and made the cheese right here in Paris, our shipping costs would be lower and we could undercut those Emmentaler so-and-so's. Do you have a place in mind to make it?"

"I have a wealthy woman friend. She's a fan of all things Roman. In her backyard she has a large granite trough once used to water Caesar's horses. We could clean it up, you know, sterilize it, and make the cheese there."

Some of what Esau said made sense; the rest was madness. But he had a track record of facilitating the careers of my literary friends and was somewhat of a mentor to me so I said I'd help.

Next day we went to five cheese shops looking for Bel Paese. In heated, offended tones the cheese merchants asked us why we wanted an Italian cheese when there was plenty of fine French cheese to be had. One woman gave us a sample of *Bleu du Vercors-Sassenage*; a gentleman offered us a taste of *très cher Beaufort* — both delicious cheeses but not something that would get our poet friend out of the Champs-Élysées McDonald's and onto the shelves of a French book chain.

When our operation was finally set up, we found it took six to eight weeks for the cheese to mature. The first batch was a little crunchy because someone had forgotten to get all the tiny pieces of granite out of the trough. So we lined it with sheeting but the cheese tasted of plastic. Finally, we got it right and sold enough Bel Paese to the restaurants and Croc-monsieur vendors to spring our poet friend from his honorable but greasy job. Our reward came when his first published poem, "The Waste Basket," received the prestigious Prix de Staples.

Here then is the first stanza. Witness the prescience of Esau and the genius of Laidlow.

August is the hottest month, feeding
Tourists eat of the sidewalk, sandwich
Hunger pangs vs. diet pledge, fighting
Root beers with ice cream.
Heat for janitor Jean, cleaning
Broom in sweaty fingers, sweeping

A little brush to cracked goobers.
Sprinklers surprised him, smoking Gauloises
the butt of lung jokes
Came the shower of wet; we wondered what
the hell's that,
But moved on to greatness, walking the Tuile-
ries,
And popped oxys, and slumped on our bench.
Hey girl, kinda Russian, wanna sell me your Pop-
up Blocker?
Or how 'bout Doktorskaya on a nice roll,
Mine tante, she made me sandwich, crummy,
And I no like it. I said, Auntie,
Vanya, throw this out. And out it went.
Of Jean's errands, janitorial.
He must waste the basket, if he does not fill it
full. ®©

———

The French have many wonderful sayings. This is
my favorite:

> *Le fromage est debout seule.*

> The cheese stands alone.

ADVICE AND GETTING AWAY

People would come up to me in cafés and ask for advice while I was writing. The first thing I'd say was "never bother a writer while he's working." Since almost no one took that advice I had to come up with points like "use the word 'truck' as much as possible because that's how people speak today." I'd give an example: "Get the truck out of here." If there were a decorative sword hanging on the wall, I'd take it down and ask, "Do you know how a plucking chicken executioner offs a yardbird with one slicing, artistic kosher stroke? May I show you?" Then they'd run. If anyone stayed I'd let loose with some real advice: Keep sentences short. See? Don't be seduced by dashes — and; semicolons. If you can leave out something important like _____ or _____ and your reader senses what's been left out, that's better than blabbing on and on and on. I'd also shared my theory that it's necessary to get out of town every once in a while. It's rejuvenating.

When I got home my wife had packed our suitcases, my knapsack, and a little bag for Mr. Thumby's things: his bottles, diapers, and a rubber pacifier in the shape of the 'thumbs up' sign. I was hoping it would bolster his self-esteem and keep him from sucking his own thumb. When I sensed he was coming into his own, I'd drop Mr. Thumby and call him by his real name: Cuthbert.

Train stations. Putting up with the din and the bad air and the expensive sandwiches was the price you paid to leave Paris. We were going to a little town on the Franco-Austro border called *Schmantz-an-Peaseporridge*. No one could find it and that attracted me. Schmantz made a wine called *Schlägt den End-darm* that was rated at 18 percent alcohol. To give you a sense of comparison based on what's available in supermarkets, Pinot noir is generally 13.5 percent and zinfandel is 14 percent. Many commercial white wines are lower. Pinot grigio — I can't even feel it.

We boarded our train and got Thumby settled. My wife opened a hiking magazine and I pulled out *Winemaking for Novices*. I was deep into the history of the rare Addoraca grape when the conductor sang out our stop. Steam engulfed us as we stepped off the train and a friendly porter was waiting to take our bags.

"*Mein Name ist Uwe.* You are going vhere?"

Since most of Austria spoke German I went with the 'v' substitution of the 'w'. "*Vir sind auf die Schmantz Hilton gehen.*"

"*Das ist gut.*"

"Ve came for the vine."

"*Auch gut.*" [Also good.]

He loaded our luggage into the Hilton courtesy van. I gave him a small tip and we left the railroad station.

My wife and I were soon checked in, relaxing on beds filled with eiderdown. Mr. Thumby played on the floor with one of his toy bulls.

"I'm going to the bar to relax for a while," I told my wife.

"Save some for the rest of us," she replied with either lightness or sarcasm. I didn't stop to find out which and headed downstairs.

The wooden banister was smooth, worn by thousands of hands: good hands, bad hands, clean hands, dirty hands, hands without wedding rings, hands with severely bitten nails, hands that couldn't wait to hold a drink.

The bar was small but it didn't matter; the wine glasses were the right size. I sat at a tiny table. A diminutive woman in her late teens came over to me.

"What are you, about four-eleven?"

"*Ich bin eineinhalb Meter hoch.* You vish to order?"

"What's that wine you have that's so special?"

"You mean the Schlägt den Enddarm vine?"

"What's that mean, anyway?"

"It means 'kicks your rectum.' "

I didn't know whether to laugh or be on heightened alert for incontinence. I ordered a bottle. While I was waiting I stared around the room. Stuffed deer heads with long antlers looked back at me with dead glassy eyes. When the end came, I wondered, were they surprised, angry, or relieved? My wine arrived.

"I pour?" asked the waitress.

"Sure, go ahead."

She poured the first glass without spilling a drop. Those Austrians are certainly neat, I thought. Did they get that from the Germans or was it the other way around?

The wine was damn good. I tasted raspberry, vanilla, some kind of herb, and tomatoes. I poured another glass and tried not to think about writing. By doing close to nothing, my subconscious arroyo would refill. New plots, fresh characters, vivid scenes, and stuffed animal heads would speak to me with their stories of sportsmanship or brutality. All I had to do was drink more.

The cuckoo clock on the wall chirped five cuckoos. That meant it was time to get my wife and have dinner. I stood up, lost my balance, grabbed the chair, and righted myself. I made a note to order another bottle of this wine with our main course.

When I got to the room, my wife was dressed and the baby had been bathed and was ready to go. Anherst took my arm and we walked downstairs into the dining room. Dinner at five is early any-where except Delray Beach, but I wanted to maintain the wine buzz I'd begun. A different waitress came over, greeted us, and suggested the *Tafelspitz*.

"And a bottle of 'Kicks Your Ass.' "

The waitress giggled at first and put her hand over her mouth to stifle the sound but could not help breaking into knee-slapping laughter. There was no maître d' so the bartender came over to see what was going on. The waitress whispered something in his ear and with all his Tyrolean might he hah-hahed until his eyes teared up. He composed himself and turned to my wife.

"The lady vould like this also?"

My wife nodded.

The laughter started all over as an avalanche of hilarity overcame the entire party, burying us in mirth and the mystery of some ancient bacchanalian rite. The bartender waddled over to the wine rack, pulled out the requested bottle, uncorked it, let me sniff, and offered it to my wife who declined. He poured for the table. I was in such a good mood I offered a glass to the bartender and waitress. Both of them gave the international "no thanks" sign made by waving your hand at a ninety-degree angle to your arm. They were still laughing as they walked back to their stations.

"I think it's pretty good," my wife said, "but I've never had a wine that tasted of tomato."

"Well, it's an old recipe. Did you know most wines were conceived to pair with certain foods? Let's ask the waitress."

I called her over.

"Miss, my wife and I were wondering what this wine was made to go with?"

With raised eyebrows she answered, "Orgies." This is going to be an adventure, I thought, and poured us both another glass.

The Tafelspitz was delicious: beef boiled in a broth of root vegetables until tender, served with potatoes and an apple-horseradish sauce.

Maybe we had another bottle of Schlägt den Enddarm. What I do remember is being carried back to my room by the burly bartender. If my wife and I made love I don't remember that either. But I do have one surviving memory:

At about four in the morning my gut started hurting. I felt pressure, jumped out of bed, and trotted down the hall. Mt. Etna erupted. Vesuvius flowed burning lava. Krakatoa did its worst.

Next morning at breakfast there was no break-fast. Our waitress had left a note for the morning staff. A happy little blonde with pigtails came to the table carrying an aperitif glass filled with a green liquid.

"What's that?" I asked.

"Something you need."

"Yes, yes. What's in it?"

"I don't know."

"Well then what's it called?"

"*Beruhigt den Darm.*"

"And what does that mean?"

"I'm not sure I'm translating this right, but Uwe says it means 'soothes the colon.'"

THE OTHER SIDE OF
SNAKEBITE

I think it's time for the truth. Everyone talks about the negatives of being a drunk or binging. There is another side to that coin and I'm here to flip off the experts.

Start with blackouts. Where else can you forget your troubles and get happy for six to eight hours. Not enough in that special account to pay your taxes? Blame someone else. Editors botch your work? Ditto. A matador you cared about get gored? Double ditto. Think maybe you eviscerated a loved one? E = screw that squared. Futuristic films show memories eradicated with flashing lights surrounding your head? Blackouts are much simpler.

If you have a pussycat personality, drinking can turn you into a lion. Therapy to make you more assertive can be expensive. How much is a bottle of Jim Beam?

True, booze can also have the opposite effect. It can cause one to be withdrawn and anti-social. Good. Those people were not contributing to society. Let them weep into their Alexandrian goblets because there were no more wine bars to conquer.

Besides, why be negative? Sometimes you need to drop to the very bottom before you can begin your long climb back to self-deception. Alcohol will do that for you.

And in the end, the ice you take is equal to the drinks you make.

PIZZA MY MIND

And her note read, "I want you to leave. I want a divorce. I've had it! The hell with you" and there was no period at the end of the sentence, indicating this was ongoing.

My wife had TiVo'd the marathon rerun of three year's worth of television shows about a meth dealer, meth users, the cops that chase them, and the women they lie to. On Saturdays, when I didn't work, we'd watch until I had a headache: relentless episodes about the magnetic pull of addiction, family bonds, weakness, strength, obsession, love, hate, betrayal, and expectations that could never be met. She said to me, "I drink because you drink," and I said, "Another alcoholic's excuse. Another droopy reason." Somehow, I thought that watching the life-smashing effects of addiction would make an impression on her. But although we'd just seen all this horror on TV and I'd stopped drinking for nine days, it didn't matter. On Sunday afternoon she went out and bought her normal dose of pain-killer: three twelve-packs that sometimes grew to five.

While I was gauging my reaction to all this, I thought of the ancient symbol of the wheel of fortune from the tarot cards: the head of a man (thinking about sex), the head of an eagle (eyeing dinner), the head of a bull (stubborn), and the head of a lion (will eat your ass when necessary). Maybe I didn't understand the admixture of symbols but I knew one thing: I was not the master of my emotions. I had not transcended the situation. I had rejected acceptance, and I was forever tortured by the results of that darkness like Prometheus chained to a rock where an eagle daily pecked his liver — the origin of chopped liver, actually — so "everything is good."

Meanwhile, Marcel, our little white poodle, had chewed a hole in a pillow. Bits of white feathers stood in relief against our blue armchair. Did my imbibing wife think the dog was going to clean up after himself? Was there much difference between a meth sty and a sot sty? From one who's cleaned them both, the answer is "no."

As they may have said on *Family Feud,* "Show me 'resentful husbands.' " I needed to get out of my compartment for a while to cool down. But I made a wrong decision as to where to go: Costco. My first errand (because my wife's TV shows took precedence over doing errands) was to refill the ink cartridges for my printer. Fifteen dollars at Staples for a recycled cartridge, ten dollars at Costco for a refill. But there was an unexpected added price: time. And as Ranceford Rolex once said, "Time is money."

At first the woman behind the counter told me, "Two cartridges will be ready in one hour." I filled out the paperwork and paid. Then she said, "It will take an hour and twenty-five minutes and I'm doing you a favor."

There was no way I could spend close to ninety minutes in a French Costco pushing an empty shopping cart in front of the *foie gras* display, or chilling by the low-sugar absinthe pop suckers. I wasted another twenty minutes staring at thirteen varieties of frozen pizza. My mind went numb with choice anxiety. Angrily, I bought a bottle of wine that said 15 percent alcohol and went home.

After the gulpin' I began to calm down. In addition to my wife's inability to do errands, I was inundated with hatred scenarios going 'round my head as I recalled the drive back from the world-wide discounter. Road rage issues resurfaced despite the fact that Yom Kippur had just passed. Apparently that forgiveness routine doesn't work for everyone.

The thirteen-dollar bottle of wine was a let-down — it disappointed me like my high school girlfriend, Jezebel, only in a deeper way.

But everything's good, right?...like pogroms, forced marches, rigged elections, and Jezebel. What clarity I found in the middle of that bottle.

COILED SPRING

Many years ago, my sponsor from a self-help organization advised me to go to an AA meeting. I sat next to a tall, late-twenties blonde with excellent posture. I felt her tension — like a tightly wound spring. At any second, if the wrong thing was said, I knew the spring would be sprung and this woman would drink again.

At the front of the room, speakers came and went, confessing "slips" or relapses. One woman said, "I was in Düsseldorf on a business trip. My hotel room came with a minibar. My boss had put pressure on me to make more sales. Something inside me snapped and I thought, I'll just have one Stoli to relax. When I woke up, all the little bottles in the baby fridge were empty and I had eight slices of braunschweiger between my toes. I hate to waste food so I saved them for my boss."

But there were many success stories and the audience would clap. After a moment of silence, everyone joined hands, and the meeting adjourned. Younger women hit on older men, and people put way too much sugar in their hot drinks. The blonde came up to me and said, "You want some coffee?" I told her, "Caffeine keeps me awake but I love this delicious French chocolate" and stuffed some in my mouth. The blonde, still tense, said, "Did you know that chocolate has caffeine in it?" I was so mad at myself I went for a drink and she joined me.

DICK'S HARDWARE

I hadn't seen him for a while, mostly because of his wife.

"What's bothering you, Fitzy?" I asked.

"It's very personal."

"Well, we're sitting here alone at a café where no one knows us. There's no need for a wiretap but look under the red candle anyway, would you?"

"I don't see anything."

"Okay so we have complete privacy. Go."

Fitzy's mouth was half-closed in a pensive look of distress. I knew some secrets about momentum and walked over to the bar.

"Waiter. We'd like two Drambuies." (Like thick scotch with sugar syrup — the gateway liquor for Jack Daniels.)

By the time I sat back down, the deft waiter was setting drinks on the table.

"*L'chaim,*" I toasted and added, "Erin go bra-less." Fitzy threw his drink back like a practiced Irishman. I sipped mine and asked, "So what's up?"

"That's a good question. Emelda doesn't think much of my manhood."

"What?"

"She says I'm small."

"Well, that's not true when it comes to your tipping."

"Right. Thirty percent should be fine, and if the service sucks, nothing sends a message like twenty percent."

"Back to your equipment," I said. "What exactly is her problem?"

"Can I have another drink?"

I made that happen, he swallowed and continued, "She says she doesn't feel anything."

"Your wife is so blotto by the time you go to bed, she wouldn't feel birth."

Fitzy brought up a point. "I thought I was average or maybe a little below average. What's average anyway?"

"According to my father's medical books, six inches when you're browsing *Playboy* and less when you're not."

"One more drink," said Fitzy, "and then I have a special request."

I started to get defensive. "I will not be interfered with."

"That's not what I mean." He motioned to the waiter for two more drinks and drank both. Now came the hard part. "Would you measure me?"

"No, of course not." I could feel myself getting huffy.

"Well then, how about if I ask the bartender for a European yardstick?"

"And he watches us stroll into the men's room with a yardstick?"

"So?"

"A micrometer would work."

Fitzy's face went white.

"Just kidding" made a bit of color return.

While I was getting the drink I should have had that Fitzy scarfed, a solution came to me. I sat back down, reached into my pants, and plopped something onto the table.

"Is that what I think it is?"

"Yes, Fitzy, I've had it since I was a boy. It's a small tape measure from Dick's Hardware in the town where I grew up. See, it's got the address and phone number on it. Good promotional tool, huh?"

"I guess."

"You take this into the *pissoir* and check yourself out. I'll wait here. And don't forget to wash it off."

"No. You need to come with me. You'll have to testify to Emelda next time we get together."

"Why don't you ask the bartender to text a notary public. Maybe they could even stamp your thing for you...and initial it."

Fitzy could be manipulative and said, "I'll buy the whole bottle of Drambuie, pay the tab on all the drinks we've had so far, and you come with me and just watch. Look, Ma, no hands! No walks on the wild side. Deal?"

We got up from the table and entered the badroom. I handed him the little tape measure and he did what he had to do. On the way back to the table I was whistling and glanced at the bartender to see if he suspected anything. He didn't; I was just paranoid. We sat down. Silence.

Fitzy spoke first. "Are you hungry?"

"I could eat."

A chalkboard with the specials of the day sat on an easel near the bar. He put on old battered glasses and squinted. We ordered oysters.

After dinner I got up, brushed cracker crumbs off my lap, and waited for him to pay the tab. Fitzy reached into his pocket, pulled out some bills, and grew pale again. His words still echo in the men's room of my mind:

"I'm a little short."

THE MOST SELF-DEPRECATING
WRITER EVER

I'm not going to name him because his heirs would be embarrassed. But if you lived and worked in Paris in those years you'd remember him as the most self-deprecating writer ever.

Low self-esteem can do horrible things to a person. If you were constantly criticized as a child you have a start to it. Never being praised doesn't help either. And if you chose a profession off-limits to your dreams — the diagram of which is an isosceles triangle where a precious few get to the top and striving masses yearning for a royalty check populate the bottom — you may act out the unfulfilled way you feel or become an alcoholic or go mad or get angry in traffic.

The worst thing he did was to print out his work on 3-hole punch, take a dog leash, put the clasp through the upper left-hand hole, and drag it through the streets of Paris in front of everyone yelling, "Careful. Don't step on it!" We didn't know if he was taking his story for a walk or felt so little pride in his work that he would belittle carefully wrought words by dragging them through mud puddles and over burning cigarette butts and discarded wads of bubble gum.

The second worst thing — for some people harder to take — was to hear him tell war stories:

"I sat in her reception area for an hour. Her secretary paged her and then tried her two cell phones. No answer. How freaking rude is that? Make an appointment and then duck it? I left. And did she or her secretary call to apologize or reschedule? No."

He told that story over and over until other writers stopped sitting with him. We passed the hat once and bought him fifty minutes with a psychologist. It did no good so it's true what they say: "The nebbish is impervious to therapy."

Modesty was taken to new limits. I'd compliment him on a beautifully composed sentence and he'd say, "I didn't really write it. My arm and hand are just vessels for my muse."

"And who is your muse?"

"Erato."

"Isn't that the proofreaders' muse?"

"I wouldn't know. I never get that far."

Then he'd take his dirty, soiled manuscript off the café table, hook the dog leash back into the ragged hole that — at the very least — needed one of those gummed reinforcements to keep it from tearing completely, thank me for the drink I bought him because he was usually broke, drop his papers, and drag them across the floor and out the door.

His funeral was appropriately held on a cold, gray, rainy day. As seen from the heavens, five umbrellas in tight formation created a black dome. He had carefully saved and paid for a tombstone. His name was not on it nor the dates that he lived. The inscription simply read:

He took a sad song and made it worse.

THE MAN WHO WROTE WITH MARKS-A-LOT

Black squiggles were the talk of Paris. They were everywhere: on buildings, lampposts and billboards. At first they struck me as nothing more than the imp-work of a twelve year old boy: goatees and mustaches added to the forlorn faces of models selling cold cream or ice cream. A week later, eye patches were added and then clumsy Dr. Frankenstein stitches on the forehead. When a cartoon balloon appeared with one word — HELP — I didn't need a Freudian to tell me this was a cry for you-know-what.

He was not a graphic artist or even a tagger; he was a poet. I found this out through another Thesaurean who discovered one of his masterpieces in a Belgian children's magazine — a poem so profound and far-reaching I'm compelled to share it:

Eensy weensy spider went up the water-
spout
Down came the rain and washed the spi-
der out
Out came the sun and dried up all the rain
Now the eensy weensy spider went up the
spout again

What insight on persistence! What a distillation of fate and fighting back! And yet this genius who'd bettered many a high school haiku received no credit or royalties from this poem — or lyric if you will —sung by children around the world. What a letdown.

Fueled on meth for the energy, oxy for the pain, and ecstasy for the synapse destruction, the man would zip around the city in the early morning hours brandishing his Marks-A-Lot like Zorro. A few quick strokes and he'd vanish into the dawn.

After weeks of witnessing the quiet madness that obscurity can bring, I felt I had to do something for him. There in the Yellow Pages under "Poets" was his information. My first visit did not go well. He wouldn't let me in. But I went back with the business card of an entertainment attorney and shoved it under his door. By visit three he was hopping mad.

Although we had never been formally introduced, he came right to the point as we talked through the door: "The lawyer wants a thirty-five hundred dollar retainer just to start. I don't have that kind of money."

"What can I do for you, then?"

"Bring drugs."

"But you'll die if you keep this up."

"Good. That's a solution."

I didn't want to be preachy but I had to tell him: "You know 'thou shalt not kill' from the Ten Commandments? It also means thou shalt not kill thyself."

"That's deep. And don't forget 'it's okay to say no to drugs.'"

I got what he was saying and I knew he heard abdication in my voice when I asked, "What do you want?"

"Whatever you can get me. And no shrinks. If I can't get the recognition I deserve for 'Spider' (that's what he called it) then living in fog is my choice."

This was very sad to me. I walked away from his web-filled apartment and decided to do nothing. A few months later I brought Mr. Thumby to a birthday party and heard lines from "Eensy Weensy" sampled on a child's rap record playing on a little girl's iPad. I took a drink.

Sitting in my regular café a year later, a mutual friend came up and said, "Did you hear the news? Your old friend, Sir Marks-A-Lot, cleaned up. He went back to school, studied industrial chemistry, and patented his own, cheaper version of Wite-Out. You can get it at Staples. It's called Blotto."

FALL

Then Came Bronson: Michael Parks as a catalyst for change riding a Harley-Davidson through episodic TV. "Then Came You": a song by the Spinners. Then came fall.

In Paris the temperature drops in September; you need a jacket when you go out at night. I haven't lived everywhere but I can tell you that a Paris fall is somewhat like a New England fall or a Michigan fall. The cold on your face is exhilarating after the steamy, humid, mosquito-biting hell of August and I welcomed this season like a thirsty *poivrotte* [female tippler] welcomes a free rum and Pepsi.

Once in the seven years I lived in Paris, fall didn't come; we just skipped from the end of a long hot summer to Christmas. We didn't even have Thanksgiving. There was Santa ringing his bells, asking for money, and it was only Labor Day.

Weird. Someone decided the economy needed an early boost.

When I was in the States at the end of October I found I really missed European Halloween: hundreds of six-year-old Napoleons working the rue Elba, occasional Dukes of Wellington not getting much candy, Louie XIVs in expensive outfits, Marie Antoinette zombies staggering, holding their heads under their arms, Richard III with feather pillows creating the illusion of poor posture, Ivan the Terrible, Ivan the Worse Than Terrible, and Ivan You Won't Believe This Guy roaming the arrondissements of Paris copping lollipops, Tootsie Rolls, and fondants from the well-to-do. When the moon was full and you had that *Claire de Lune* pale light that Debussy hopefully witnessed and then put to music, the scene was an odd combination of gruesome and cute.

The year the Paris fall didn't come was like breakfast without orange juice.

When world climate issues cooperated and fall did come, I switched from sitting inside to an outdoor table at my favorite café. It was really cool outside, hundreds of people walking by dressed in the latest styles, some wearing pretentious scarves. If the scarf was too long and someone stepped on it, the wearer cried "eeeuh" and the cruel giggled.

I would drink hot things when I sat in the cold. Coffee was good but you needed to fortify it with cognac. When winter got closer I would order a hot toddy — leave it to the alcoholics to make drinking sound cute. If you were ever a professional singer, the benign version is easy to remember: honey, lemon, hot water, and a tea bag. The hardcore add whiskey or brandy. On Christmas day and only on Christmas day, my café would serve a drink called *Sex for Santa.* The recipe was top secret but I could taste crumbled Red Hots, Russian vodka, lemon zest, crushed ice, and the graininess of a five-milligram nerve pill. I had four of these frappés one year, became very relaxed, and let my mind wander:

Sledding out of control down an icy slope, bashing my head into an elm tree, blood trickling down my forehead, a bandage improvised from a dirty pretentious scarf, infection, antibiotics, a painful scar, the apple pie I made Santa — rejected because it gave him heartburn — candy canes hung on a perfect tree, electric shock from frayed colored lights, homemade tinsel from newspaper, that small fire, the confusing menorah, sitting on a maroon carpet in pajamas opening presents, a fireplace that was never lit, a clown uncle, the dry microwave turkey and the gravy that saved the day, mashed yams topped with tiny marshmallows, chocolate-covered cherries, my first insulin shot, all the pies and cakes you could eat, out of breath from being overweight, sneaking green crème de menthe from the liquor cabinet, attracting like-minded people, marriage, the end of sex, the infinite joy of being greeted and loved by a dog.

I went home to recreate that good doggie fix. After five straight minutes of licking and kissing and tickling and petting, I sat down and looked at the fall leaves blow by my window and thought a good name for a rock group with a smart audience would be the AutumN Empire.

HUNGRY FOR THE BAYOU

Walking around Paris can be exhilarating; its architecture is timeless. Honey locust trees line the streets. The Louvre can cheer you with beauty or overwhelm you with that same beauty. And a walk along the *Boulevard Saint-Michel* with young Sorbonne students checking you out can put back a bit of the excitement marriage can take away. But it's maddening to see people walking and eating a hot pressed sandwich called a *Croc-monsieur*. It's maddening because you're hungry and you smell the crispy good French bread, béchamel sauce, melting cheese, and crocodile meat. Diners walk and munch, walk and munch. And you're hungry and jealous, hungry and jealous.

I should have had a granola bar before I left the house but I was stupid and skipped the most important meal of the day. But I had tricks. I could bite my nails or I could think of food smells that

126

disgusted me like liver. Then as I left my low-rent neighborhood with no businesses, I'd gradually come upon the shiny plate glass windows of bakeries, charcuteries, and liquor stores. If nobody was looking, I'd lick the window feeling like Tiny Tim in front of a toy store. Denied because Tim's father worked for a cheap-ass who wouldn't share the wealth. Denied a simple freakin' little Christmas present because of circumstances beyond his control. Like me. Poor me.

You dirty, freaking, complaining, absinthe-loving nutcase. Didn't you learn anything when your best mercenary friend, Chunk, told you not to complain, to keep everything inside? No one asked you to become a writer. You went into it of your own free will and it's just a matter of time before you earn a good living at it. Until then, put Tiny Tim and his Dickensian deprivation out of your mind. Don't think about the Croc-monsieur. Think about writing something the public wants. And next time, eat the granola bar.

I walked past the rest of the shops and temptations. But there was one more little distraction to overcome. The new lower-fat Burger King French fries had just come to Paris and lovers were feeding them to each other along the Champs-Élysées. They smelled good so to bolster my resolve I conjured up Chunk and his favorite thing to say: "Get it together or I'll rip you a new belly button." I conquered my hunger and went to a café.

Almost empty. Good. At the bar just a *pirouette* — a ballet dancer who didn't make the big time. She taught for drinking money. I tried to frame her situation with compassion and philosophy: Accept G-d's wisdom.

I ordered. The cursor on the screen of my laptop blinked. I blinked. The first sentence of a new story I would call "On the Brink of Distinction" came to me. I named the file and started typing.

THE PORTUGUESE CAFÉ

Although I had my regular café, sometimes I found new places. This was my second time at the Portuguese café. As before, the women and girls who served me were charming, friendly, and attentive. The Caesar salad was perfect — balanced so you tasted lemon, Parmesan, and a hint of anchovy.

One of the waitresses looked like a girl I dated many years ago. That brought back satisfying memories.

Spanish guitar duets played in the background. I ordered *sopa de pedra*. It was very good and when I added a pat of butter it became spectacular. The menu said the soup had ten vegetables in it. I began counting: carrots, kale, cabbage, kidney beans. Part of the soup had been pureed with an electric wand so I think onion, garlic, potato and turnip had disappeared into the good thick broth.

It bothered me that I could only taste eight out of ten vegetables. Ah, parsnip! That was probably in there for sweetness, then discarded. Maddeningly, I had only guessed nine out of ten ingredients. And isn't life like that. Sometimes there's lightness, kindness, and grace but somehow you bask in the bitter. I was working on overcoming that.

I had eaten light — or, if you will, lightly — so there was room for one of their desserts. The bakery section in its great wisdom offered tarts the size of a silver dollar called *natas* (pronounced na-tash). The sweet pastry crackled in your mouth as you chewed. The filling tasted like a cross between custard and crème pâtissière, the filling for an éclair.

Chandeliers lit the back room and became brighter as the afternoon sun went down. A couple at the next table thanked everyone for such a nice meal as they left. And for me, this lovely Portuguese café gave that feeling of well-being I always wanted but rarely found when I ate out. I had no wine and everyone in the place was beautiful.

ON THE BRINK OF
DISTINCTION

At one time I read books on metaphysics. The deal was to acquire such-and-such arcane knowledge, apply it, and things you wanted in your life would manifest. One book told of a man who was almost out of money. The book advised him to use his last dollars to buy an expensive coat. He did, and sudden wealth came to him because he believed it would and people — seeing him in the fine coat — thought he was loaded.

Another book with esoteric secrets from either India or New Jersey told the reader to picture his or her desire, surround the image with a pink bubble, and release it into the universe for fulfillment.

The last metaphysical book I studied was an ephemeris tracking the movements of the planets. You took the information that Jupiter was trining

Mercury, looked up the meaning in another book, and acted on it. One day I was trying to make an appointment with a publisher, talking to his secretary.

"I need to see him on March twenty-third," I insisted, based on the position of the planets.

"We can't do the twenty-third," she kept repeating.

"Why? I'm available all day."

"Because, Mr. Author, the twenty-third is a Sunday."

That wrapped up my interest in all things metaphysical. If these principles work for other people, I say, "Go for it," although as I read recently the Jewish Torah does not condone any of these practices.

Since it takes one to know one — and I freely admit I was one — I can tell you the shyest people are the ones who really go in for metaphysics. They go to psychics instead of conferences. They throw the *I Ching* instead of their weight around, and they look at the material world like a smorgasbord where they don't even have to get in line to get fed; just imagine what you'd like to have on your plate and magical waitress Desiree brings it to you. The day this works you'll see the streets overrun with Porsches and Mercedes. Disease will be history.

So after buying into this way of thinking with no results, I tried some realistic approaches that required me to leave the house, meet people, sell myself and my work, and make deals. I signed a publishing agreement with Scribblers based on assurances that they had the resources to upload my book to Kindle Central.

But I didn't want fame because I saw the high price celebrities paid to have it. I didn't need a mansion as heating and cooling that many cubic feet adds up. But we did need a new kitchen because tile is so hard to clean with all those little grooves.

I was a writer who loved to write and would someday solve the mystery of the ages: grease, mum, or bird is the word.

HERE FISHY FISHY

Almost everyone I know who is rich or wealthy came upon their money in one of three ways: they inherited it, they worked hard for a short time, or they did something underhanded to get the ball rolling. If you inherited a bundle then good for you if you did good things with the money. If you persevered for a few years, hit the jackpot, and grew your stash — yippee. But if you manipulated or cheated people or the system, I have a problem with that because I benefited. I sat in your box seats looking properly contemplative and mingled at your self-service receptions not knowing about the tainted fount of your Miller High Life.

I was led to you by the hybrid son (half WASP-half Inuit) of a successful importer of Chinese ipecac. He knew how to tie an ascot and how to convince me to come along on meaningless escapades: bird watching in London pubs, rating snow bunnies in

Zermatt, singing background vocals on crap records in Hollywood, and as bow-tied window dressing for charity balls where the proceeds disappeared into a cloud of overhead. In typical rich person fashion, he also knew how to explore the working class.

It was as if he wore a cloaking device that hid his filthy moneyed ways. And in those seemingly innocent drunken dawns, midmornings, and early afternoons, I couldn't see the harm that was being done.

When he was out hustling, his babysitter — he was the baby — stayed with us in our hut in Tortuga. While Anherst tutored the local children, the babysitter got nervous about her homework. Hortense was twenty-two. I solved her math problems and created my own: What does one plus one plus one equal? Trouble. She made me want to redefine the word "morass." And it was all his fault.

In the spring when the snow started to melt he foresaw poor skiing, guiding us to Cuba for the rum festival. That fall as unionists were crushing inequities in Upstate New York, there was Steinbeckian wine to quaff. And as winter cycled through again, he introduced us to a knockoff of the Iditarod in Alaska using uncooperative moose instead of huskies. Finally, I saw through the icy smile of this user of animals and people and let the social climber scale Magic Mountain without us.

I HEAR YOUR NAME, I LEAVE FOR MAINE

The cowbell of time was beating in my head. I wasn't sure if it was the intro to a song by the Rolling Stones or the Chambers Brothers but I did know that my good sense was urging me to get out of town.

I had married a six-year-old. Of course she wasn't really six years old but in the kitchen she acted like it. A robot maid was needed to follow her around cleaning every spill, wiping the stove of stew, washing dishes she left in the sink for three days, sweeping the floor, and windexing chocolate handprints off the light switch. Unfortunately, I was the robot.

There, I hear her in the kitchen right now. She's spooning out a second helping of bean salad and grunting. Now I have to go and clean up after her for the fifth time today. Just a moment. Just a moment.

Okay no spills this time but a drawer was left open. See what I mean?

My father used to say to me, "Don't sweat the small stuff," and I knew that lack of tidiness was trivial but it was still confounding that my wife had been raised by wolves. But like a good wolf mother she was compassionate to her kin, loving, and faithful. Not everyone gets that. And she was beautiful. It was as if I had married Michelle Williams, Charlize Theron, and Scarlett Johansson all rolled into one. But with beauty can come problems and as her husband those problems affected me.

There are people — walking around or shuttered in dark bedrooms — who are severely affected by loss. My wife took several years to get over her grandmother's death and never recovered from her twin brother's passing. And even though her bad seed, crackhead niece made Patty McCormack look like Desmond Tutu, when the niece died an Irish wake began that had no end.

Things would get so bad around the house I would pack a fresh T-shirt, stuff a feather pillow into a bag, and take the train out of Paris where motel rates were cheaper. Since there was nothing I could do about her problem, submitting to the will of the universe was the only balm for a wound that never healed. Then I'd return home and my wife would be contrite for a day. When her next binge began and

I drank too, the absurdity of our situation grew like bamboo. Again I packed my bags.

———

The state of Maine has a lot to recommend it: reasonably priced lobster, steamed clams, fried clams, Italian sandwiches.* James Taylor and John Travolta have homes there. A fish called scrod, sweet scallops, free coleslaw when you know where to go, puffy fried onion rings, salt water taffy, sweet corn that was not genetically engineered, milk that tasted a little like grass, and blue caps with a big red "B" for Boston Red Sox fans.

Pine trees, four seasons, the Atlantic ocean, shrimp you can trust, soft sandy beaches, Monet-like fall colors, people who mean what they say, skiing, a provincial outlook that's both refreshing and frustrating, too many fried foods, the Protestant work ethic, dated liquor laws, micro brews, crisp Cortland apples, okay cell reception, clouds.

I didn't go to Maine. You can't run from love because love always finds you. And I was ready to be true.

---

* On a twelve-inch freshly-baked roll are placed slices of boiled ham or Genoa salami or turkey, white American cheese, bits of Greek olives, sour pickle spears, slices of green pepper, chopped onions, tomatoes sliced directly onto the sandwich, salt, pepper, and olive oil.

Stories That Weren't Good Enough

BE HAIR NOW

When my wife and I saw two Japanese artists at Googi's salon with their long straight shiny black hair, we said to each other like a couple of goofy school kids, "Let's do that!" It didn't occur to us that if your hair was naturally wavy you wouldn't get the same Japanese results. Then we saw a BBC clip on the Rolling Stones; there was Brian Jones in his dressing room with his hair in big curlers. So that's how he got that long smooth look — he was cheating. Not manly as far as I was concerned. I lost sleep wondering if any of the Beatles used that trick. Counter-combing was all right with me, but curlers? That was a girl thing.

We found a quiet corner of the gathering to discuss our newfound hair plans.

"Let's both cut our hair so it's the same length," my wife suggested.

"What if our hair grows at different rates?"

"Then we'll trim it."

"How long do you think it will take to look Japanese?"

"Nine months to a year."

"That's too long."

"What if we got hair extensions?"

"That's for poseurs."

"What if the poseurs had implants?"

"That's a question for the ages."

Even though I'd been drinking, I had a sudden burst of clarity: This hair stuff was ridiculous. It was a waste of time talking about it but I couldn't say that to my wife. There were some things I knew about women and this was one: Don't belittle cosmetology.

———

When I had the chance, I slipped off to a Paris hotel where I had a large Oscar de la Renta trunk stored in the basement. I took the folded-up print-out of the hair story from my sport coat pocket, put it carefully in the trunk, locked it, and returned to my evil café where I could think up a better story.

I was into a good bottle of *Barolo* when a thought occurred to me: I hope the hell when I'm gone and someone finds that trunk, they have the good sense never to publish *Be Hair Now*. What good would it serve? Maybe it was a cutesy insight into the private world of my wife and I, but talking about hair and curlers and extensions was such a contrast to the public image I was cultivating of writing and drinking, I wished I'd burned the silly thing but all my work was precious to me and I saved everything — even if it was cacaesque.

I took out my iPhone, tapped "voice memo," and whispered so no one in the bar could hear me: "Note to future publishers. Cut hair story."

TEACHING MY SON ABOUT WOMEN

Even though he was two years old, if he retained a fifth or a tenth of what I taught him, that would be good, and I felt like when Mr. Thumby got out into the world he would know more and not make the same mistakes I had made because he didn't understand women.

We were in the Jardin du Luxembourg, a magnificent public park in Paris, sitting on a comfortable wooden bench watching a man and woman in their twenties having a heated discussion. I couldn't hear what they were saying but their body language and facial gestures told me much and I wanted to pass my observations on to my son.

"Here's a gen-er-al-i-za-tion I want you to remember, Thumby. Women need to vent and men want to problem-solve. Do you see how that emotional woman's hands are gesticulating? And that spot between her eyebrows...do you see that it's crinkled? Those are signs she's troubled and emoting. Now look at the man. He looks frustrated, right? That's because he's offering up solutions to solve the woman's problems. He's too young to know that all she wants is for him to listen. Can you imagine saying to Mount Saint Helens, 'Don't spew' ?"

My eyes scanned left to another scene. "See the guy asking that girl out on a date? He's trying way too hard. He's scaring her. Linking up with women is a delicate balance of interest and restraint. There, did you see her touch her hair? That's a good sign. That's what's called body language. In this case that move implies interest on her part."

Mr. Thumby pointed to another couple sitting on the bench next to us so we could hear them. I had the sense they were casual friends, not lovers. The guy asked very nonchalantly, "Do you wanna see a famous French film?" and the girl instantly got tense.

"Did you see what just happened, Thumby?" He shook his little head "no." "When a guy asks a girl to do anything, even if it's innocent with no intent of anything behind it, many girls will take that as a come-on. They're going to think "he wants something, he likes me, he wants me." Beware of that one, son, it can get you in all sorts of trouble."

"And here's something for your twenties. When you're checking out a female, don't let biological pressure be the only determining factor. Try to look into the future and ask yourself these questions: What's the mother like — "That's *Mrs.* Gorgon to you" — and how much damage did she do to the kid? What's the girl's religion? If she's a Buddhist and you're a Methodist, how do you think that's all going to play out Sunday morning? Do you see any red flags like early signs of alcoholism (she motions to the waiter for large flagons of beer when dinner is long over), drug abuse (she says she's going to Marseille for soap and comes back with an industrial drum of muscle relaxers), overeating (waist *ipsa loquitor*), or depression ("I hate you. Get out.") If any of those things cropped up after marriage, could you live with them for a lifetime? After all, you've made a vow. Thumby?"

My two-year old had gone to sleep so I didn't know how much of what I said had fallen on deaf ears. I could only trust in the power of the subconscious.

I woke him and we decided to walk. I bought my boy a vanilla ice cream cone. A beautiful woman walked by, made eye contact with both of us, and smiled. My son frowned because he didn't understand what was going on. I explained. "You just witnessed an example of 'maternal instinct.'

That gal was actually attracted to both of us — to you because she wanted to mother you and to me because I've been vetted in a way. She knows I can father a child, feed him, clothe him, and nurture him. Women love that. Social anthropologists will tell you these feelings go back to the time of the caveman (*One Million Years B.C.*) and Raquel Welch. The Neanderthal has to prove his worth, hence all those family movies where a guy pretends to have a kid when he really doesn't, just so he can get the girl."

"Any questions?"

"Burp."

"Just one more thing, son. Don't tell Mommy about this."

THE DOG WHO DID NOT LIKE WALKS

People didn't believe me when I told them I have a dog that does not like to go for walks. All dogs love walks, right? Not this one. When Marcel's acute doggie hearing picked up the jingle of the leash or he saw me putting on my sneakers, he would run away and hide. Refuge was behind my wife's head on her pillow in bed.

Like a parent who knows his child should go to school even though he doesn't want to, I would approach Marcel holding his harness. He'd growl at me and that was the only time he'd growl except when we were playing tug-of-war with a blue squeaky ball. I knew he wouldn't bite me because poodles are a polite breed. They're also very smart. Marcel sensed that treats like bones and chew-toys would stop if he ever took a chunk out of my hand.

All I knew to do was hitch him to his harness while he was protesting, clip on the leash, and start tugging — a tug to get him off the bed, a tug to get him to the front door, a tug to move him out the door, a tug to encourage him down a few stairs, and a tug to get him onto the sidewalk. Now the smell-a-thon began.

He'd smell the flowers the landlady planted. He'd walk up and down a tiny patch of grass — sniffing but not "going." I'd firmly say, "Marcel, go potty." With no results that command would turn into a question: "Marcel go potty?" Still nothing. So we'd start our walk.

I loved being outdoors. I've had life-bracing adventures that took me around the world so naturally I expected my dog son to feel like me. He didn't. Nor did he have the ancient instinct that was bred into him: routing out small animals. Squirrels didn't bother him, or pigeons. "Live and let live," that was Marcel's credo. But get him near another white poodle and "yap yap yap, bark bark bark, whine whine whine"; Marcel became the Ronald Reagan of dogs: the Great Communicator. He'd sniff, allow himself to be mounted, crouch, pounce, and forget for a moment that he didn't like walks.

Some people teach their dogs to say, "I love you." I once heard a Doberman do it. To amuse folks on our walk I taught Marcel to say, *ra-ra-Ra-ra-ra*, (then slower) *Ra-RA-ra-RA*. ["Mr. Gorbachev, tear down this fence."]

When we came upon people, he'd really open up. Being a small dog he had a routine. Those who didn't like dogs called it "jumping up"; dog lovers called it "hugging." "Oh, he's hugging me," this sweet Filipino woman used to say. I could see his paws wrapped around her leg and became convinced this was a sign of deep affection. We also met shih tzus, scotty dogs, Jack Russell, a pit bull and his heavily tattooed owner who would graciously cross the street, and a bichon frise who stood a little taller than Marcel.

By the time we had gone three blocks you would think that Marcel would remember how much fun this was, but when we turned to go home, strong gusts of wind were hard on the little dog and he'd pant.

Once inside our warm home, I'd take off his harness and leash, he'd shake himself to rid his body of that controlled feeling he apparently disliked, prance up the stairs to the second floor landing, and relieve himself. I didn't understand any of this but like a forgiving grandparent who's grown too tired to scold, I let it pass.

———

Everyone has something different that warms his heart, that resonates with what he considers good and beautiful. For some it's art. For others it's architecture and a perfectly painted wall. For me, the most beautiful thing in the world is to see a dog smiling.

It was like
a toy looked in my eyes
came alive
and then kissed me.

HILARIOUS TOMASSINO

There are at least two ways to frame bullfighting: It is brutal, bloody, and cruel; or it is cultural — man vs. nature, bravery beyond comprehension, and juicy steaks for uncommitted vegetarians at the end of the day. I'm not informed enough to debate both sides of the issue but I do know a funny matador when I see one.

"*Él hizo reír al publico.*" [He made the crowd laugh.] That's what they put on his tombstone and the reverence or irreverence the masses showed him consisted not of flowers, but hand buzzers, chewing gum that turned your lips and mouth black, sneezing powder, dozens of colored handkerchiefs tied together that he pulled out of the bull's ear, and a blinking red plastic clown nose that used to infuriate El Toro. Yes, my friends, he was unique in his game, a hybrid, an amusing matador who truly learned in front of hundreds of fans that death is easy — especially in the afternoon — but comedy is hard.

His story begins in "Barthelona," where it sounds like you're lisping but you're not — you're just pronouncing "c's" in the proper way. Nevertheless, he was teased by outsiders, taunted by the moronic, and spat on by the phlegmatic. Conditions like these can produce a future serial killer or the opposite — someone who learns to kill audiences (metaphorically) with pathos, oversized shoes, and a Superman cape.

His first appearance was not an accident. His adopted father, Shawn Diego, was getting tired of his son's bad impressions of Rodney Dangerfield. One day while they were in the front row at a bullfight, Diego pushed his twelve-year-old boy into the ring as a mother bird will push her baby out of the nest to see if it can fly. And fly he did.

Once in the ring, Diego's son came alive to the life he was meant to have.

With no fear he went right up to the bull, and pinching a line he once heard said, "I tell ya, I don't get no *respeto*." The bull looked puzzled, shook his head, and the crowd went wild. *"Hilarante Tomassino"* [Hilarious Tomassino] they yelled. And that's all it took for the show biz bug to enter his being. The die was cast. Caesar crossed the Rubicon. Edison electrified the world. Moe slapped Curley and got a laugh.

No one had ever seen a matador put a pie in the face of a bull. Nor had they ever seen a matador blow sneezing powder into those large black nostrils. But Hilarious did this and more. A hand buzzer that might have jolted you in grade school took the place of the tricky cape flourish known as a "veronica." Bulls didn't know what to make of this. They were confounded, shook their heads, and made the cutest little grunt — their version of "huh?"

Tomassino was not a svelte man like most matadors but he did wear the traditional garb except for one thing: sewn on his posterior was a picture done in red sequins of the most despised dictator in South America. He took terrible chances sticking his butt in the bull's face and it was brave — even though he never played that dictator's country.

His Humpty Dumpty belly almost always popped the buttons of his tight-fitting outfit and brought a rousing *olé* from members of the crowd on spartan diets. As you might have guessed, the more the bull had to work with, the more goring that went on. But the gut of Hilarious Tomassino was like a bulletproof vest and all his wounds were superficial. The care and feeding of that tum-tum was something to behold.

One night at dinner I watched him put away three baskets of chips, six servings of salsa, three double margaritas, and a large guacamole meant for a table of eight. Then they brought the main meal: a five-pound steak (free if you could eat the whole thing, and he did), papas fritas, mole, and a back-up carnitas burrito in case he was still hungry. And apparently he was since he disposed of the burrito like a sword-swallower and then asked, "What's for dessert?"

The waiter whose mouth and lips were twitching with value judgments set two healthy portions of flan on our table. This was the first time I did not see Hilarious smile. His eyes narrowed into the chilly stare of an Old West gunslinger. He pursed his lips and said nothing for an uncomfortable minute while the waiter deduced the order through logic, intimidation, or ESP.

Five minutes later, our server reappeared with two busboys who cleared the table. The waiter motioned toward the swinging doors of the kitchen and a grinning, obsequious chef brought out an entire pan of flan. I estimated the size in American inches at eighteen by twenty-four.

Now looking pleased, Hilarious picked up a soupspoon and began shoveling flan into his mouth at the pace of a county fair pie-eating contest. He motioned for me to push the yellow painted bowl of whipped cream in his direction. I did, still thinking, why hadn't he offered *me* any flan? I like flan.

In this province of Spain, flan is traditionally served with a maraschino cherry. So a bowl of cherries appeared with the waiter offering to spoon some onto the dessert. Hilarious patted him on the back, sent him on his way, put the bowl up to his mouth, and started sucking. (I had read in one of my father's medical textbooks that not being breast-fed could have consequences in later life.) The slurping sounds were embarrassing but other diners were now gathered around laughing, so this must have been part of Hilarious's comedy.

When the ambulance arrived and the attendants started defibrillating, Hilarious was fighting, stuffing handfuls of whipped cream into his pockets for later. It made a mess but helped quiet him down.

The hospital staff put in an IV line that Hilarious ripped out, started sucking on, and spat. "This is salt water," he protested as if it should have been maple syrup. I explained to him about saline solutions and he flopped back on his gurney, exasperated.

He survived the ministrations of doctors, nurses, and the hospital's dietician, lost eight pounds (dinner?), and went home where he immediately put a green folding beach chair in front of his opened refrigerator and began to eat himself to death because he didn't like to be told what to do. His maid said he was laughing the whole time.

Today, when you visit a bullring where this matador fought, you'll find that other matadors have adopted some of his moves. When sneezing powder makes the bull explode, you can hear the crowd roar halfway across the city: *"Hilarante, Hilarante."* And sometimes, if you're quiet, you'll hear *"te bendiga"* which means "bless you."

MY DINNER WITH ANDRÉ
THE SEAL

I once shared a vegan meal with Herb the Bull in Barcelona hoping to get his side of the story. And there was that picnic in Plombier Park with Adam Ant. Those occasions went well. But I was nervous about eating with a seal who may have had a grudge.

Seated at a back table so as not to attract attention, I noticed it was just 8 p.m. when André flopped in. He saw me, honked, and made his way to my table. He got up into his chair like a character from Tod Browning's disturbing film, *Freaks*. But André was not a freak; he was a seal — a semi-aquatic mammal — and a movie star. I hoped to learn something about seventy-one percent of the earth's surface.

We all know people can talk to animals and vice versa. Dr. Dolittle proved that. Eye movements, gestures with the head, low growls, high-pitched barks indicating excitement, clapping, and possibly ESP are all ways man and non-man communicate.

The first message I got was "How's the fish at this place?"

"Try the salmon," I said.

André shot back, "Those f*ckers. Spawn, spawn, spawn. I will not eat the young."

"How 'bout calamari?" I asked.

"Do you know how intelligent squid are?" I can't bring myself to chow down on someone who could have been in MENSA. Herring. There's a *fehrcactah* fish. No common sense, no *saychel*. I wouldn't mind a plate of herring. Clean up the ocean of stupidity."

I ordered for us both. The waiter brought a glass of light red wine for me and a saucer for André. He lapped up his drink and I could tell he was getting a buzz because he started in.

"Eskimos. Those mother f*ckers. Can you believe those guys? My sweet little cousin...clubbed to death for food and her fur and blubber. Do you know how much fat a baby seal has? Not much! Inuit f*ckers."

I replied with as much compassion as I could. "Hasn't seal meat been a source of food for the Eskimo for thousands of years, and don't they take only what they need?"

"Let's switch places," said André, nodding his head and twitching his whiskers. "How would you like it if, for instance, the Swiss had a tradition of eating Americans? Can you dig it? Maybe they'd take a hunk off your ass and call it 'Swiss steak.' Do you feel my pain, brother?"

André needed another drink, got the waiter's attention, and motioned with his head toward his saucer, much like a trained horse. Wine came and he lapped. I sipped because I could and noticed André turning from one shade of black to another. An eruption of pissed-off-ed-ness was building. Then he yelled, "Sea World!" I knew I was in for it, simply because I was a man and he was a seal.

"Zoos are so wrong," he fumed.

I drank a little more wine. "How about the argument that they're saving species from extinction?"

"I don't know if that theory has ever been proven. And although I'm sad for the fallen trainers, why do you think giant whales go bad? They don't want to be in f*ckin' captivity. Much like married men."

André had stumbled on a truth that caused him to start snorting — his version of laughter.

When our fish arrived, he gobbled the whole thing in a few seconds, licked the plate, then clapped with his flippers.

"I guess you liked it," I commented.

"F*ckin' great. Délicieux."

"So you've picked up some French living here in Paris. What's the word for 'seal'?"

"*P-h-o-q-u-e*. Phoque."

THE NO SOLUTION SOLUTION

My thoughts went back to all the problem drinkers I've known. Who had recovered? A middle-aged businessman had stopped drinking cold turkey. No programs — willpower. Someone my age was a delightful drunk so I didn't notice that he had a problem called "beer for breakfast." Then he told me he'd started going to AA. Not all the guidelines were followed but he did stop in a significant way with only a drink now and then. A third person I knew had a long-term relationship with malt liquor. He'd get into his car at lunchtime, scooch down so no one could see him, and drink his drink. The love of a good woman — which he'd had before — finally did the trick.

I ran into another good woman — a very wealthy woman I used to know. She was shopping in a high-end grocery store, beautifully attired in an all-white cotton summer dress. Eating from a plastic container of Pacific Palisades papaya, she offered me some.

"How's your family?" I asked.

"You remember my oldest and youngest sons?"

"Yes."

"They're both at Oxford."

"And your middle daughter Maya?"

Without missing a beat she replied, "She's in her ninth rehab."

I remembered a Polaroid I'd taken of the family: Maya had a mischievous smile like Shakespeare's Puck.

We parted amicably, not asking for each other's contact information. I continued shopping with two words going 'round my head: nine rehabs.

At a Polish café that night I started to draw some conclusions: If someone wants to stop drinking, they will. It might depend on will power, it might depend on G-d or a program, or it might depend on having a reason to stop such as "they're going to take away my kids unless I stop drinking" or "I'm going to die if I don't stop drinking."

Then there was the other side. Comfortable seats in bars. Hands touching hands. The pleasant din of conversations bouncing off a polished concrete floor. Flattering lighting.

Back home my wife was binging. She had entered her moaning and talking-to-herself stage. I had left the house angry because she put a wet-bottomed beer bottle on a piece of furniture that was made during the Civil War. But that's the draw: you stop caring about things and you especially stop caring about yourself. It's tempting to dance into the void — the void where G-d created all things.

AN UNFORESEEN EPILOGUE

I need to comment on the contents of this book in light of the fact that I am now going to AA.

It's a verifiable fact that Parisian Reasons was 100 percent written and 80 percent edited before I got into trouble with the law and began to attend meetings at the behest of my attorney.

The AA-related anecdote about the *braunschweiger* from chapter 19, "Coiled Spring," was fictionalized from an episode fourteen years ago when I was in a companion organization and my sponsor suggested I attend an AA meeting to see if there was anything I could learn. Over time, I learned to be a better man, just not that day.